To my mother, who without I never would have learned of our great detectives in literature and art.

Contents

Murder On The Royal County Course

Chapter One

There is, I believe, a well-known anecdote about an aspiring young author who, very eager to begin his story with an impact sufficient to seize the attention of even the most jaded editor, wrote the dramatic opening sentence:

"'Hell!' said the Duchess."

Curiously enough, my own story opens in much the same manner, though the lady who made the exclamation was certainly no duchess.

It was an early June morning. Having concluded some business matters in Liverpool, I was returning on the morning train to London, where I still shared lodgings with my good friend Rupert Mulligan, a former British detective.

The Kings Cross express was remarkably empty; indeed, my compartment had only one other occupant. I'd left my hotel in something of a rush, and was still busily checking to ensure I'd not left any belongings behind when the train moved off. Until that moment, I had scarcely noticed my travelling companion, but I was now suddenly reminded of her presence. Jumping abruptly from her seat, she lowered the window, thrust her head outside, and then, withdrawing it quickly, uttered a brief yet emphatic, "Hell!"

Being somewhat old-fashioned, I prefer a woman to maintain a certain femininity. I confess I have little patience for the modern neurotic girl who dances from dawn to dusk, smokes incessantly, and employs language capable of making even a Liverpool fishwife blush.

I glanced upwards with mild disapproval at her pretty, mischievous face beneath a daring little yellow hat. Thick chestnut curls covered her ears. She appeared to be barely seventeen, although her face was powdered, and her lips unnaturally red.

Entirely unabashed, she met my gaze directly and performed a mock grimace.

"Oh dear, we've shocked the respectable gentleman!" she said dramatically, addressing an imaginary audience. "My apologies for the language—most improper, of course—but, heavens, there was good cause! Do you realize I've just lost my only sister?"

"Really?" I responded courteously. "That's unfortunate."

"He disapproves!" the young lady announced dramatically. "Utterly disapproves—of me, and my sister—which is hardly fair, as he's never even seen her!"

I attempted to speak, but she interrupted briskly.

"Say nothing more! Nobody loves me! I'll retreat to the garden and eat worms! Boohoo, I am but devastated!"

With that, she hid behind a large humorous Irish newspaper. However, within moments, I noticed her eyes peeking stealthily over the top. Despite myself, I smiled slightly, prompting her to toss aside the paper and burst into a merry fit of laughter.

"I knew you weren't as stern as you looked," she declared.

Her laughter was so infectious I couldn't resist joining in, though privately I found the term "stern" mildly disagreeable.

"There, now we're friends!" she proclaimed cheerfully. "Say you're sorry about my sister—"

"I am profoundly sorry!"

"That's a good chap!"

"Allow me to finish," I said gently. "While I'm indeed very sorry, I think I'll manage quite comfortably without her company." I offered a slight bow.

However, this unpredictable young woman frowned and shook her head vigorously.

"No, drop it. I rather liked your 'dignified disapproval' act. Oh, your expression was perfect—'definitely not one of us,' it said. Quite right, too, although these days it's harder to tell a duchess from a chorus girl. There now, I've probably shocked you again! You're fresh out of the backwoods, I'd say. Not that I mind. We need more of your type. I loathe men who act familiar; they infuriate me."

She shook her curls energetically.

"What happens when you're furious?" I asked, smiling.

"I'm an absolute terror! I say and do whatever pleases me. Once I nearly finished off a man. Truly. And he'd have deserved it."

"Well," I said quickly, "please don't get angry with me."

"I shan't. I like you—did from the first moment I saw you. But your disapproving look made friendship seem unlikely."

"Well, now we're acquainted. Tell me about yourself."

"I'm an actress—not the sort you're probably thinking of. I've been on stage since I was six years old—tumbling, you know."

"Pardon me?" I asked, puzzled.

"Ever seen child acrobats?"

"Oh, I see!"

"I'm American by birth, but I've lived mostly in England. We have a new act now—"

"We?"

"My sister and I. Songs, dances, comic routines, mixed with acrobatics. It's novel, and audiences adore it. We expect to make good money."

She leaned forward enthusiastically, speaking rapidly and using theatrical expressions that were largely incomprehensible to me. Nevertheless, I found myself increasingly intrigued by her. She seemed both worldly-wise and naïvely sincere, utterly determined to succeed.

We passed through a crossroads where a Royal Army truck was waiting. The sight brought back many memories, and my companion seemed intuitively aware of my thoughts.

"Thinking of the War?" she asked.

I nodded quietly.

"You served?"

"Yes. I was wounded once, during the retreat at Sollum in Africa. Eventually, I was invalided home. Now, I'm something of a private secretary to an MP."

"My! That's impressive!"

"Not especially. There's very little to do, just a few hours daily. Quite dull work, actually. Fortunately, I have other interests."

"Don't tell me you're a bug collector!"

"No, I share rooms with a fascinating individual—a British ex-detective, now working privately in London. He's been remarkably successful, solving cases that baffled official authorities."

Her eyes widened in excitement.

"How intriguing! I adore crime stories, movies especially. And when there's a murder reported, I'm absolutely glued to the papers."

"Do you remember the Dornoch Case?" I asked.

"The elderly lady who was poisoned in the Scottish Highlands?"

"Yes. That was Mulligan's breakthrough case. Without him, the murderer would have escaped entirely."

Enthusiastically, I recounted the highlights, culminating in Mulligan's remarkable and unexpected resolution. The girl listened, utterly engrossed. We were both so absorbed that we barely noticed when the train pulled into Kings Cross.

I secured two porters as we stepped onto the platform, and my companion offered her hand.

"Goodbye, and I'll mind my manners better from now on."

"Oh, but let me look after you on the boat."

"I may not take the boat—I must find out if my sister got aboard elsewhere. But thank you."

"Surely we'll meet again? Won't you even tell me your name?" I called after her as she moved away.

She turned her head briefly. "Belle," she laughed, disappearing into the crowd.

Little did I suspect under what circumstances I would encounter Belle again.

Chapter Two

It was exactly five past nine the following morning when I entered the sitting room I shared with Mulligan, ready for breakfast. Mulligan, as punctual as ever, was delicately tapping the top of his second boiled egg.

He glanced up, beaming at my arrival.

"You slept soundly, yes? Recovered from your terrible journey across? Marvellous, you are almost punctual today. Ah, but your tie—it lacks symmetry. Allow me to correct it."

Elsewhere, I've already described Rupert Mulligan. An extraordinary little fellow! Height, five feet five inches precisely; head shaped somewhat like an egg and carried slightly to one side; eyes that flashed ice-blue when excitement overtook him; a pointed goatee beard, and an unmistakable air of enormous dignity. He was always impeccably neat—dapper, even. Indeed, neatness bordered upon obsession for him. The sight of a tilted ornament, the smallest speck of dust, or any slight disorder in attire was sheer agony to Mulligan until he'd set matters right. His devotion was to "Order" and "Method." He harboured a mild contempt for tangible clues—footprints, cigarette ash, and the like—insisting firmly that such things, alone, never solved any case. At such moments, he would tap his egg-shaped head, absurdly pleased with himself, and say with supreme confidence: "The true detective work occurs here, within. The little grey cells, remember always the little grey cells, my dear friend."

I took my seat, remarking casually to Mulligan's greeting that a train ride of barely over four hours from Liverpool to Kings Cross hardly deserved to be labelled as "terrible."

"Anything interesting in the morning mail?" I asked.

Mulligan shook his head with evident dissatisfaction.

"I have not yet looked through my letters, but nothing interesting arrives nowadays. The great criminals—those masterminds of crime—they no longer exist."

He shook his head sadly, and I laughed heartily.

"Cheer up, Mulligan, your luck is bound to change. Open your letters. For all you know, there could be an extraordinary case waiting."

Mulligan smiled faintly, and taking his neat little opener, methodically slit open the envelopes by his plate.

"A bill. Another bill. I am becoming extravagant as I age. Ah—a letter from Wood."

"Yes?" I was instantly attentive. The inspector from Scotland Yard had previously led us to several intriguing investigations.

"He merely offers his thanks—in his own unique manner—for the minor point I corrected him on during the McNairn Case. I was pleased to assist."

Mulligan resumed his placid perusal.

"A request to lecture to our local troop of Boy Scouts. The Baroness of Guildford would appreciate my visiting her— doubtless another missing lapdog! And now the final letter. Ah —"

I lifted my head swiftly, noticing the change in his voice. Mulligan was reading with deep concentration. A moment later, he passed me the page.

"Now, this is intriguing, my dear friend. Read it yourself."

The letter, written boldly on distinctly foreign stationery, read as follows:

Royal County Golf Course, Magennis,
Northern Ireland.

Dear Sir,
I require the services of a detective urgently and, for reasons I will disclose later, cannot involve the official police. Your name has reached me from various sources, all agreeing on your capability and discretion. I hesitate to share details by mail, but due to certain information I possess, my life is in constant peril. The danger, I feel certain, is imminent. I beg you, therefore, to lose no time in travelling to Northern Ireland. A car will await you at Belfast if you wire ahead with your arrival details. I must ask that you set aside any other cases and dedicate yourself solely to mine. You shall be generously compensated. Your involvement may be necessary for some time and may include travel to Barcelona, where I spent several years. Name your own fee, and it will be met.

Assuring you again of the urgency,
Yours sincerely,
M. W. Foley

Below the signature was hastily scribbled, barely legible, the line:
"For God's sake, come!"

I handed back the letter, my pulse quickening.

"At last!" I said. "Certainly something out of the ordinary here."

"Indeed," replied Mulligan thoughtfully.

"You will accept, of course?" I pressed.

Mulligan nodded, clearly deep in thought. Finally deciding, he glanced at the clock. His expression was unusually solemn.

"My friend, we must lose no time. The Liverpool express leaves from Euston at eleven. Do not worry—we have sufficient time, ten minutes for discussion is permissible. Will you accompany me?"

"Well—"

"You mentioned your employer doesn't require your services in the coming weeks."

"Oh, that's fine. But this Mr. Foley clearly stresses the confidentiality of the matter."

"Ta-ta-ta! Leave Mr. Foley to me. By the way, his name seems familiar."

"There is a wealthy Irish-Spanish millionaire named Foley, though I'm not sure it's the same man."

"But undoubtedly it is. That explains Barcelona. Barcelona is in Catalonia, Catalonia is part of Spain! Ah, splendid, we are making progress! Did you notice the postscript? How did it strike you?"

I paused, considering.

"He clearly wrote the letter carefully controlled, but lost composure at the end, impulsively adding those desperate words."

But Mulligan shook his head vigorously.

"You are mistaken. Notice, the ink of the signature is dark, yet the postscript ink is faint."

"Well?" I questioned, puzzled.

"My dear friend, use your little grey cells. Is it not obvious? Mr. Foley wrote his letter calmly, reread it without blotting, then deliberately—not impulsively—added the final desperate line, only afterward blotting it."

"But why?"

"Precisely to evoke the reaction it had upon you!"

"What?"

"Exactly—to ensure my immediate attention. He reread his original letter and found it lacking urgency!"

He paused, adding quietly, his eyes sparkling with that peculiar gleam of internal excitement:

"And therefore, my friend, as this postscript was added soberly, deliberately, the urgency is genuine, and we must hasten to him without delay."

"Magennis," I murmured thoughtfully. "I believe I've heard of it."

Mulligan nodded.

"A quiet, yet fashionable place, located midway between Belfast and Dublin. Does Mr. Foley maintain a residence in England?"

"Yes, in Chelsea, I think, and a larger country estate in Kent. Though I don't know much about him socially—he keeps to himself. I believe he has substantial business interests in Spain and Portugal, having spent considerable time there."

"We'll soon have the full story from Foley himself. Come, let us pack quickly. A small suitcase each, then a taxi to Euston."

Eleven o'clock saw us aboard the train departing Euston for Liverpool. Before leaving, Mulligan dispatched a telegram informing Mr. Foley of our imminent arrival.

"I'm surprised you haven't invested in a supply of seasickness remedies, Mulligan," I remarked mischievously, recalling our earlier conversation at breakfast.

My friend, who was anxiously scanning the skies, turned a reproachful gaze upon me.

"Is it possible you have forgotten Mitte's most excellent method? I always practise it religiously. One balances oneself, if you recall, gently turning the head from left to right, breathing deeply, counting six between breaths."

"H'm," I murmured sceptically. "You'll be thoroughly tired of balancing yourself and counting to six by the time you reach Barcelona—or Lisbon, or wherever you finally land."

"What an idea! You surely do not imagine I will travel all the way to Barcelona?"

"Mr. Foley suggests as much in his letter."

"Mr. Foley was not acquainted with the methods of Rupert Mulligan. I do not dash from place to place, exhausting myself. My investigations take place here," he said firmly, tapping his forehead.

As usual, this claim triggered my argumentative nature.

"That's all very well, Mulligan, but you're beginning to underestimate certain practicalities. A fingerprint, after all, has often led directly to the arrest and conviction of a murderer."

"And has undoubtedly also sent more than one innocent man to the gallows," Mulligan replied dryly.

"But surely you admit the importance of detailed investigation—fingerprints, footprints, cigarette ash, different soils, and other minor clues—?"

"Undoubtedly. I have never denied their usefulness. The expert observer indeed has his value! But others—the Ruperts Mulligans—stand above the mere experts! Experts collect facts; the task of men like me is to interpret the crime itself—the logic behind it, the sequence and significance of these facts, and above all, the true psychology involved. You have hunted foxes, have you not?"

"I've joined a hunt occasionally," I admitted, slightly puzzled by this abrupt shift. "Why?"

"Well, in this fox-hunting, you require dogs, yes?"

"Hounds," I gently corrected. "Certainly."

"But," said Mulligan, wagging his finger emphatically, "did you yourself leap from horseback, sniffing the ground and barking loudly 'Ow Ow'?"

Despite myself, I laughed aloud. Mulligan nodded, satisfied.

"Precisely. You leave the job of dogs—hounds—to the hounds. Yet you expect Rupert Mulligan to lie down, perhaps on damp grass, scrutinizing hypothetical footprints and scooping up cigarette ash, though I cannot distinguish one type from another. Remember the Midlands Express mystery. Inspector Wood eagerly set off to inspect the railway tracks. When he returned, without leaving my apartments, I could tell him exactly what he had discovered."

"So, in your opinion, Wood wasted his time?"

"Not at all. His findings merely confirmed my deductions. But for me to go would have indeed been a waste. It is similarly the case with so-called 'experts.' Consider the handwriting specialists in the Beauchamp Case. One side highlighted similarities, the other pointed out discrepancies. All highly technical, and to what result? Merely confirming what we already knew—that the handwriting resembled Philip Beauchamp's. Yet the psychological question remains 'Why?' Was it truly his writing, or had someone purposely imitated it? That question, my dear friend, I alone answered—and correctly."

Having effectively silenced—though perhaps not entirely convinced—me, Mulligan leaned back contentedly.

On the boat, I refrained from disturbing my friend's solitude.

The weather proved delightful, the sea as tranquil as the proverbial millpond. Thus, I was not at all surprised when a cheerful Mulligan rejoined me upon our arrival in Belfast. There was, however, disappointment awaiting us, as no vehicle appeared to meet us, which Mulligan attributed to a delay in his telegram's arrival.

"We shall hire a car," he announced optimistically. Shortly thereafter we were rattling and jolting along in possibly the most ramshackle automobile ever offered for hire, bound for Magennis.

My spirits soared, yet my little friend regarded me with a solemn expression.

"You are experiencing what the Scots call 'feyness,' Lockhart. It foretells misfortune."

"Nonsense! At least, you don't seem to share my high spirits."

"No," he admitted quietly. "I am uneasy."

"Uneasy about what?"

"I cannot say precisely. But I have a premonition—a deep instinct." His seriousness affected me despite my scepticism.

"I sense," he said slowly, "this case may be complicated—a long, intricate puzzle difficult to unravel."

I would have pressed him further, but we had just reached the outskirts of Magennis. We slowed to inquire directions to the Golf Course.

"Straight ahead, sir, through town. The Royal County Golf Course is about half a mile further. You can't miss it—a big clubhouse overlooking the sea."

We thanked our informant and proceeded, soon leaving the small town behind. At a fork in the road, we halted again, noticing a peasant trudging toward us. Awaiting his approach, I observed a tiny, dilapidated building beside the road, obviously not our destination. As we waited, its gate swung open and a young woman emerged.

The peasant reached us, and our driver leaned forward to question him.

"The Royal County Golf Course? Just along the right fork ahead, sir. You'd see it clearly if not for the bend."

The driver thanked him and restarted the engine. Meanwhile, my eyes remained fixed upon the girl, who stood with one hand resting lightly on the gate, watching us pass. I appreciate beauty, and this was a girl no one could fail to notice. She was tall, possessing the graceful bearing of a young goddess; her uncovered head shone golden in the sunlight. I privately vowed she was among the most beautiful girls I had ever encountered. As the car ascended the rough road, I turned my head to gaze after her.

"By Jove, Mulligan," I exclaimed impulsively, "did you see that goddess?"

Mulligan raised his eyebrows in gentle amusement.

"Again!" he murmured. "Already you've glimpsed a goddess!"

"But, good heavens, wasn't she?"

"Possibly, but I didn't particularly notice."

"You must have seen her!"

"My dear friend, two people seldom notice the same things. You, for example, saw a goddess. I—" He hesitated briefly.

"Yes?"

"I saw only a young woman with anxious eyes," Mulligan said quietly.

At that precise moment, we arrived at a substantial green gate and simultaneously uttered exclamations of surprise. Blocking our way stood a stern-looking Ulster police officer. He raised his hand in a commanding gesture.

"You cannot pass, gentlemen."

"But we're here to see Mr. Foley," I insisted. "We have an appointment. This is his golf course, isn't it?"

"Yes, sir, but—" he began uncertainly.

Mulligan leaned forward sharply.

"But what?"

"Mr. Foley was murdered this morning."

Chapter Three

In an instant, Mulligan sprang from the car, eyes blazing with excitement.

"What is this you say? Murdered? When? How?"

The Ulster policeman straightened up stiffly.

"I'm sorry, sir. I cannot answer any questions."

"Quite so. I understand." Mulligan paused to reflect. "The district inspector, he is inside, no doubt?"

"Yes, sir."

Mulligan drew out a card, hastily scribbled a few words, and handed it over.

"Would you be good enough to see that this reaches the inspector immediately?"

The officer took the card and, turning his head, let out a sharp whistle. Within moments another policeman appeared, received Mulligan's message, and disappeared into the grounds. After a short wait, a stocky, energetic man with a thick, bushy moustache hurried down to meet us. The policeman saluted and stepped aside.

"My dear Mr. Mulligan!" the new arrival called warmly. "I'm delighted you're here. Your timing could not be better."

Mulligan's expression brightened immediately.

"Mr. Blanchflower! What an unexpected pleasure." Turning to me, he said, "This gentleman is my English friend, Captain

Lockhart—Mr. Martin Blanchflower."

The inspector and I exchanged formal handshakes, and Blanchflower quickly returned his attention to Mulligan.

"My dear chap, I haven't seen you since Southampton in 1909! Do you have information that might assist our inquiry?"

"Perhaps you already know it. You were aware, I assume, that I had been summoned?"

"No. By whom?"

"The murdered man himself. He apparently knew an attempt on his life was imminent. Unfortunately, he summoned me too late."

"Good heavens!" exclaimed the inspector. "Then he anticipated his own murder? This certainly changes our theories! But come inside."

He opened the gate, and we began walking towards the clubhouse. As we walked, Mr. Blanchflower continued speaking:

"The examining magistrate, Mr. Andrews, must be informed immediately. He has just concluded inspecting the crime scene and is about to commence interrogations."

"When did the crime occur?" asked Mulligan.

"The body was discovered at about nine this morning. According to Madam Foley and the doctor, the murder likely took place around two a.m. But please, come in."

We reached the steps of the clubhouse entrance. Another policeman seated in the hall rose promptly upon seeing the inspector.

"Where is Mr. Andrews now?" Blanchflower asked.

"In the salon, sir."

Blanchflower opened a door to the left, and we entered. Mr. Andrews, the examining magistrate, sat at a large round table, accompanied by his clerk. They both looked up as we entered. After brief introductions, the inspector explained our presence.

Mr. Andrews was tall and gaunt, with piercing dark eyes and a neatly trimmed grey beard, which he habitually stroked as he spoke. Standing near the mantelpiece was an elderly man with slightly stooped shoulders, who was introduced to us as Dr. Fisher.

"Extraordinary indeed," remarked Mr. Andrews once the inspector had finished. "You have the letter with you, Mr. Mulligan?"

Mulligan handed it over, and the magistrate studied it closely.

"H'm! He mentions a secret. What a pity he wasn't clearer. We are indebted to you, Mr. Mulligan. May we rely on your assistance in this investigation, or must you return immediately to London?"

"Mr. Magistrate, I shall remain. Although I arrived too late to save my client, honour compels me to identify his murderer."

The magistrate inclined his head respectfully.

"Your sentiments are commendable. Madam Foley, I'm sure, will also wish to retain your services. Mr. Faulkner from the Royal Ulster Constabulary in Belfast is expected shortly. I'm certain you'll both provide valuable assistance to each other. Meanwhile, please join me during my interrogations. Naturally, if there is any assistance you require, it will be promptly provided."

"I thank you, sir. As of now, I am entirely in the dark, knowing nothing whatsoever."

Mr. Andrews nodded towards the inspector, who resumed the narrative:

"This morning, Rose, the elderly servant, discovered the front door ajar upon descending to begin her duties. Fearing a burglary, she checked the dining room, and finding the silver untouched, dismissed her concerns, assuming her master had risen early for a walk."

"Pardon my interruption, sir," Mulligan said, "but was that something he often did?"

"No. But Rose, like many here, holds a common perception that the English are eccentric, prone to unpredictable habits. Shortly thereafter, a young maid named Clare, entering her mistress's bedroom, was horrified to find Madam Foley gagged and bound. Almost simultaneously, word came that Mr. Foley's body had been discovered nearby, stabbed fatally in the back."

"Where was this?"

"That is perhaps the most remarkable aspect, Mr. Mulligan. The victim was found lying face-down—in an open grave."

"What?"

"Yes. The pit was freshly dug just beyond the clubhouse grounds."

"How long had he been dead?"

Dr. Fisher answered this directly.

"I examined the body at ten this morning. Death occurred at least seven, perhaps as many as ten hours earlier."

"H'm! That places the murder between midnight and three a.m."

"Exactly," said the inspector. "And Madam Foley's testimony narrows it further, placing it shortly after two. Death was instantaneous, clearly not self-inflicted."

Mulligan nodded thoughtfully as the inspector continued:

"Madam Foley was quickly released from her bonds by the terrified servants. She was in severe distress, nearly unconscious from the pain inflicted. It appears that two masked intruders entered the bedroom, gagged and bound her, then forcibly removed her husband. This information comes second-hand from the servants, as Madam Foley became hysterical upon learning her husband's fate. Dr. Fisher administered sedatives immediately, and we have not yet been able to question her. Hopefully, upon waking, she'll be calmer and better able to withstand questioning."

The inspector paused, then added:

"As for other occupants of the clubhouse, there is Rose, the elderly housekeeper, who has served here many years, originally under Lord Wallace. Additionally, two young sisters, Jenny and Clare Rankin, who come from highly respectable parents in Magennis. There's a chauffeur, brought from England by Mr. Foley, currently away on holiday. Finally, Madam Foley's son, Mr. Terence Foley, also currently absent."

Mulligan nodded in understanding. Mr. Andrews then spoke:

"McGrady!"

The Ulster policeman appeared immediately.

"Bring in the woman Rose."

McGrady saluted, disappearing briefly before returning, escorting the nervous, elderly servant.

"Your name is Rose O'Donnell?"

"Yes, sir."

"You've been employed here at the Royal County for some time?"

"Eleven years under Lord Wallace, sir. When the estate was sold this spring, I stayed on with the English gentleman. Never did I dream—"

The magistrate interrupted gently but firmly.

"Yes, yes, quite. Now, Rose, regarding the front door—whose responsibility was it to secure it each night?"

"Mine, sir. I always saw to it personally."

"And last night?"

"I secured it myself, same as always."

"You're absolutely certain?"

"I swear it by all the blessed saints, sir."

"What time was that?"

"The usual time, half-past ten, sir."

"And the rest of the household—had they retired?"

"Madam had gone to bed earlier. Jenny and Clare went upstairs with me. Mr Foley was still in his study."

"Then, if someone opened the door later, it must have been Mr Foley himself?"

Rose gave a skeptical shrug of her broad shoulders.

"Why would he do such a thing? With robbers and murderers lurking everywhere! Absurd! Mr Foley wasn't an imbecile. It's not as if he needed to let the lady out—"

The magistrate interrupted sharply:

"The lady? Which lady do you mean?"

"The lady who visited him, of course."

"A lady visited him last evening?"

"Yes, sir—and not for the first time either."

"Who was she? Did you know her?"

A cunning expression crossed Rose's face.

"How should I know who she was?" she muttered. "I wasn't the one who let her in last night."

"Aha!" cried the magistrate, slamming his hand on the table. "You would dare trifle with the police? Tell me immediately the name of this woman who regularly visited Mr Foley."

"The police—the police!" grumbled Rose bitterly. "Whoever thought I'd get tangled up with the police? But I know who she was well enough. It was Madam Wiffen."

The inspector gave a startled exclamation, leaning forward incredulously.

"Madam Wiffen—from Manor Carney, just down the road?"

"That's what I said, sir. Oh, she's a fine one, she is."

Rose tossed her head scornfully.

"Madam Wiffen!" murmured the inspector. "Impossible."

"There you are," Rose grumbled. "That's all the thanks you get for speaking the truth."

"No, no," soothed the magistrate. "We're merely surprised. Madam Wiffen and Mr Foley, they were—?" He hesitated tactfully. "That sort of thing, was it?"

"How would I know? But what do you expect? Mr Foley was a rich English lord, and Madam Wiffen, well, she was poor —though stylish enough, despite living so quietly with her daughter. She's had her past, that's certain! She's no longer young, but bless you, I've seen men turn their heads when she passes through the village. And lately, she's had plenty of money to spend—everyone in town knows it. No more economising!" Rose shook her head knowingly.

Mr Andrews stroked his beard thoughtfully.

"And Madam Foley?" he finally asked. "How did she react to this

—friendship?"

Rose shrugged again.

"Always amiable—always polite. One would think she suspected nothing. But still, the heart suffers quietly, doesn't it? I've seen her getting paler and thinner by the day. She's not the same lady who arrived here just a month ago. Mr Foley, too, had changed. He was clearly suffering from strain. And who could be surprised, carrying on such an affair so openly? No discretion, no subtlety. Purely English!"

I bristled indignantly, but the magistrate pressed ahead with his inquiry, ignoring the insult.

"You say Mr Foley didn't have to let Madam Wiffen out. Did she leave earlier?"

"Yes, sir. I heard them leave the study together and move towards the front door. Mr Foley wished her goodnight and shut the door behind her."

"At what time exactly?"

"About twenty-five past ten, sir."

"Do you know when Mr Foley himself went up to bed?"

"I heard him going upstairs about ten minutes after we did. The staircase creaks badly—no one can move about without being heard."

"And that's all? You heard no disturbances during the night?"

"Nothing at all, sir."

"Who was the first to come downstairs in the morning?"

"I was, sir. I immediately saw the front door hanging open."

"What about the downstairs windows? Were they secure?"

"Every single one. Nothing suspicious, nothing out of place."

"Very good. You may go, Rose."

Rose shuffled towards the door. As she reached the threshold, she turned back briefly.

"I'll tell you one thing, sir. That Madam Wiffen—she's bad. Oh yes, one woman knows another. She's bad, mark my words!" And with a solemn shake of her head, she exited.

"Clare Rankin," called the magistrate.

Clare arrived weeping profusely, verging on hysteria. Mr Andrews handled her skilfully. Her testimony primarily concerned the shocking discovery of her mistress bound and gagged, a situation she described somewhat dramatically. Like Rose, she had heard nothing unusual overnight.

Her sister Jenny followed. She too observed that her master had recently become withdrawn.

"Each day he seemed gloomier. He ate little, always appearing troubled."

Jenny, however, had her own theory. "It must be the Mafia! Two masked men—who else could they be? Terrible, they are!"

"That's certainly possible," replied the magistrate soothingly. "Now, Jenny, did you let Madam Wiffen into the clubhouse last night?"

"Not last night, sir. The night before."

"But Rose insists Madam Wiffen was here last night."

"No, sir. A lady visited Mr Foley last night, but it wasn't Madam Wiffen."

The magistrate, clearly surprised, pressed her further, but Jenny stood firm. She knew Madam Wiffen by sight. This visitor was also dark-haired, but younger and shorter. Nothing could sway her account.

"Had you seen this woman before?"

"Never, sir." Jenny hesitated, then timidly added, "But I believe she was English."

"English?"

"Yes, sir. She asked for Mr Foley in quite good Gaelic, but the accent, no matter how slight, always reveals itself. Besides, when they left the study, they spoke in English."

"Did you hear what was said? Could you make out any conversation clearly?"

"I speak good English," said Jenny proudly. "The lady spoke too softly to hear clearly, but I caught Mr Foley's last words as he opened the door for her." Jenny paused, then repeated carefully and slowly, "'Yeas—yeas—but for Gaud's saike go nauw!'"

"Yes, yes—but for God's sake, go now!" echoed the magistrate.

He dismissed Jenny, paused to reflect, then summoned Rose again.

He asked if she might have mistakenly confused the night of Madam Wiffen's visit, but Rose remained stubbornly insistent. Madam Wiffen had definitely visited last night. Jenny simply wanted attention, that was all—creating stories about mysterious women and boasting about her English skills! Mr Foley probably never even uttered that phrase, and even if he had, it proved nothing, since Madam Wiffen spoke English fluently and usually conversed in English with both Mr and Madam Foley. "You see, Mr Terence—Mr Foley's son—was often here, and his Gaelic was poor."

The magistrate let the point drop, instead asking about the chauffeur. He learned that just the previous day Mr Foley declared he wouldn't need the car and unexpectedly granted Masters a holiday.

A troubled frown had begun to crease Mulligan's brow.

"What is it?" I whispered.

He shook his head impatiently, then spoke up:

"Pardon me, Mr Blanchflower, but surely Mr Foley could drive his own car?"

The inspector glanced toward Rose, who promptly responded: "No, Mr Foley never drove himself."

Mulligan's frown deepened.

"I wish you'd tell me what's troubling you," I said irritably.

"Don't you see? In his letter Mr Foley specifically mentions sending a car to meet me at Belfast."

"Perhaps he meant a hired car," I suggested.

"Doubtless that is correct. But why hire a car when he owned one? Why, of all days, suddenly send away the chauffeur on holiday yesterday? Was it to deliberately keep him away before our arrival?"

Chapter Four

Rose had left the room, and the magistrate tapped thoughtfully on the table.

"Mr Blanchflower," he said after a pause, "we have conflicting testimony here. Whom are we to believe—Rose or Jenny?"

"Jenny," replied the inspector firmly. "It was she who admitted the visitor. Rose is elderly, stubborn, and clearly holds a grudge against Madam Wiffen. Besides, what we already know supports the idea that Foley was involved with another woman."

"Wait!" Mr Andrews interjected. "We neglected to inform Mr Mulligan about that." He shuffled through some documents on the table and finally handed one across to my friend. "We found this letter in the pocket of the deceased's overcoat, Mr Mulligan."

Mulligan unfolded the somewhat crumpled sheet. It was written in English, in a rather unsteady, immature hand:

My Dearest One,—Why have you stopped writing? You still love me, don't you? Your recent letters were so cold, distant—and now this silence! It frightens me. If you stopped loving me—but no, that's impossible! What a silly girl I am, always imagining the worst. Still, if you did stop loving me, I don't know what I would do—perhaps kill myself. I couldn't go on without you. Sometimes I fear another woman is coming between us. Well, she'd better be careful—and so should you! I'd rather kill you myself than let her have you. I mean every word.

But there—I'm being foolish and dramatic again. You love me, and I love you. Yes, I love you more than anything.

Your adoring, Abbie.

There was neither address nor date. Mulligan handed the letter back, his face grave.

"And the assumption is—?"

The magistrate shrugged.

"Evidently Mr Foley was involved with this Englishwoman— Abbie. He comes here, meets Madam Wiffen, and begins an affair with her. His feelings for the other woman cool, causing her to grow suspicious. This letter contains an explicit threat. Initially, Mr Mulligan, the case appeared straightforward. Jealousy! The stabbing in the back strongly suggested the act of a woman."

Mulligan nodded thoughtfully.

"The stab in the back—yes, perhaps—but not the grave! Digging a grave involves strenuous labour—physical strength. No woman dug that grave, gentlemen. That was the work of a man."

The inspector exclaimed excitedly, "Exactly! You're right. We hadn't considered that."

"As I was saying," Mr Andrews continued, "at first glance the case seemed simple, but the masked intruders and Mr Foley's letter to you complicate matters considerably. It appears we are dealing with two entirely separate sets of circumstances. Regarding Foley's letter to you, could it possibly relate to 'Abbie' and her threats?"

Mulligan shook his head decisively.

"Unlikely. A man like Foley, who spent years in adventurous situations in remote places, would hardly have sought protection from a woman."

Mr Andrews nodded emphatically.

"Precisely my view. Then we must look for the explanation of his letter—"

"In Barcelona," the inspector interjected. "I'll immediately cable the police there, asking for complete details of Foley's past life— love affairs, business dealings, friendships, and any enemies he may have made. Surely then we'll have some clue to this baffling murder."

The inspector glanced around expectantly.

"Excellent," Mulligan said approvingly.

"You've found no other letters from this 'Abbie' among Foley's belongings?" Mulligan asked.

"No. Naturally, we searched carefully through his private papers in the study. There was nothing unusual—everything appeared straightforward and legitimate. The only mildly remarkable item was his will. Here it is."

Mulligan quickly scanned the document.

"A legacy of a thousand pounds to Mr Hall—who is he, by the way?"

"Foley's secretary. He remained in England, though he visited here occasionally for a weekend."

"And everything else left unconditionally to his beloved wife, Saoirse. Simple, yet perfectly valid. Witnessed by Jenny and Rose. Nothing particularly unusual here." He handed it back.

"Perhaps," Blanchflower began hesitantly, "you didn't notice—"

"The date?" Mulligan said, eyes twinkling. "Oh yes, I noticed. Drawn up a fortnight ago. Possibly Foley's first indication of danger. Many wealthy men die intestate simply because they refuse to contemplate their own demise. But it's premature to jump to conclusions. Still, this suggests genuine affection and trust towards his wife, despite his apparent infidelities."

"Yes," Mr Andrews said uncertainly. "Though perhaps a little unfair to his son, leaving him completely reliant on his mother. If she remarried, the boy's inheritance might be at risk."

Mulligan shrugged.

"Men are vain creatures. Mr Foley undoubtedly believed his widow would never remarry. As for the son, perhaps it was prudent to leave the money in his mother's hands. Rich men's sons are notoriously irresponsible."

"You may be right. Now, Mr Mulligan, surely you would like to see the crime scene itself. Unfortunately, the body has been removed, but comprehensive photographs have been taken from every possible angle and will be at your disposal."

"I thank you for your courtesy," said Mulligan politely.

The inspector stood up. "Please come with me, gentlemen."

He opened the door, bowing politely for Mulligan to precede him. Mulligan returned the courtesy with equal politeness, each man deferring gracefully to the other:

"After you, sir."

"Please, sir."

Eventually they reached the hallway.

"That room there—is it the study?" Mulligan asked suddenly, gesturing toward the opposite door.

"Yes. Would you care to inspect it?" Blanchflower opened the door, and we stepped inside.

The room Foley had chosen as his personal sanctuary was small but elegantly furnished for both comfort and business. A practical writing desk with numerous pigeonholes stood by the window. Two substantial leather armchairs faced a fireplace, and a round table between them held recent books and magazines.

Mulligan paused, observing the room carefully. Then he stepped forward, lightly running his hand across the leather chairs, picking up a magazine, and delicately sliding his finger over the polished oak sideboard. His expression was one of complete satisfaction.

"No dust?" I teased gently.

He smiled warmly, appreciating my understanding of his idiosyncrasies.

"Not a speck, my dear fellow! And perhaps, just this once, that's unfortunate."

His sharp, birdlike gaze flicked quickly around the room.

"Ah!" he suddenly exclaimed, sounding relieved. "The hearthrug —it's crooked." Immediately he stooped down to straighten it. An instant later he uttered another sharp exclamation, straightening up with something held in his hand—a small fragment of pink paper.

"So, even in Northern Ireland—as in England—the domestics fail to sweep beneath the mats?"

Blanchflower took the scrap of paper, and I stepped forward for a closer inspection.

"Do you recognise it, Lockhart?" asked Mulligan.

I shook my head, puzzled—yet the shade of pink paper seemed oddly familiar.

The inspector, quicker to grasp its significance, exclaimed at once, "A piece of a cheque!"

The fragment was approximately two inches square, and written in ink was the name "Corrigan."

"Excellent!" said Blanchflower. "This cheque was either payable to, or drawn by, someone named Corrigan."

"The former, I suspect," said Mulligan calmly. "If I am not mistaken, this handwriting is Mr Foley's."

This was quickly confirmed by comparison with a memorandum on the desk.

"Dear me," murmured the inspector, looking embarrassed. "How could I possibly have overlooked this?"

Mulligan chuckled good-humouredly.

"The moral is simple: always look beneath the mats! My friend Lockhart here could tell you that anything even slightly askew torments me. The instant I noticed the rug was crooked, I thought: 'The legs of the chair probably displaced it when pushed back. Perhaps something lies beneath, something overlooked by our good Rose.'"

"Rose?"

"Or Jenny, or Clare—whoever tidied this room. Since there's no dust, it must have been cleaned this morning. Let me reconstruct the scene: yesterday, perhaps late last night, Mr Foley wrote a cheque to someone named Corrigan. Afterwards, it was torn into pieces and scattered across the floor. This morning —"

But Blanchflower was already impatiently ringing the bell.

Rose appeared promptly. Yes, there had been pieces of paper scattered on the floor. What had she done with them? Burnt them in the kitchen stove, naturally—what else?

Blanchflower dismissed her with a despairing wave. Suddenly brightening, he hurried to the desk, quickly checking Foley's cheque-book. His disappointment returned swiftly; the last counterfoil was blank.

"Courage!" Mulligan said cheerfully, clapping him on the back.

"No doubt Madam Foley can tell us about this mysterious Corrigan."

The inspector's face brightened again. "True enough. Let's continue."

As we turned to leave, Mulligan remarked casually, "This is where Mr Foley received his visitor last night, yes?"

"It is—but how did you know?"

"By this." Mulligan held up something pinched between his finger and thumb—a single long black hair. A woman's hair.

Inspector Blanchflower led us outside, behind the clubhouse, to a small shed adjoining the main building. He produced a key and unlocked the door.

"The body is in here. We moved it from the crime scene shortly before your arrival, after the photographers had finished."

He swung open the door and we stepped inside. Foley's body lay on the ground, covered by a sheet. With a deft movement, Blanchflower removed the covering. Foley was a medium-sized man, slender and athletic-looking, about fifty years old, with dark hair heavily streaked with grey. He was clean-shaven, his features dominated by a long, thin nose, with eyes set close together. His skin was deeply tanned, suggesting a life spent mostly beneath tropical suns. His lips were drawn back in a grimace, an expression of profound shock and terror etched into his face.

"His expression clearly indicates he was stabbed in the back," Mulligan observed quietly.

Very gently, he turned the body over. Between the shoulder blades, staining the light fawn-coloured overcoat, was a dark, circular patch with a slit in the centre. Mulligan examined it closely.

"Have you identified the murder weapon?"

"It was left in the wound," Blanchflower replied, reaching for a large glass jar from a shelf. Inside was an object resembling a paper-knife, small and slender with a black handle and a narrow, shining blade no longer than ten inches in total.

Mulligan delicately tested the discoloured blade with his fingertip.

"Good Lord! It's extremely sharp—an ideal weapon for murder."

"Unfortunately," remarked Blanchflower regretfully, "we found no fingerprints on it. The killer must have worn gloves."

"Naturally," Mulligan said with mild disdain. "Even in Barcelona they have learned that much. Even an amateur English criminal would know it, thanks to the Bertillon system's fame in the press. Still, the absence of fingerprints is interesting. It would be absurdly easy to plant another person's prints, yet our criminal chose not to. Either he was extremely cautious or pressed for time. But we shall see."

He carefully allowed the body to return to its original position.

"He wore only underclothes beneath his coat, I notice," Mulligan remarked.

"Yes," replied the inspector. "The magistrate found that curious too."

At that moment, someone knocked at the door which Blanchflower had closed behind us. He opened it quickly to reveal Rose, peering in with obvious curiosity.

"What is it?" Blanchflower asked impatiently.

"Madam sends word she is recovered sufficiently to see the magistrate now."

"Good," replied Blanchflower briskly. "Tell Mr Andrews we'll be there immediately."

Mulligan hesitated, glancing back at the body. I thought he was about to address it dramatically, vowing aloud never to rest until the murderer was caught. But when he finally spoke, his words were strangely awkward, and absurdly out of place for such a sombre moment.

"His coat was remarkably long," he observed stiffly.

Chapter Five

We found Mr Andrews waiting for us in the hall, and together we ascended the stairs, Rose leading the way. Mulligan climbed in a curious zigzag pattern that puzzled me until he whispered, grimacing slightly:

"No wonder the servants heard Foley ascending—every step creaks loudly enough to wake the dead!"

At the top of the stairs, a narrow passage branched off.

"The servants' quarters," explained Blanchflower briefly.

We continued along a corridor, and Rose knocked softly on the last door on the right. A weak voice called out for us to enter, and we stepped into a spacious, sunny bedroom. It overlooked the sea, which glittered blue and inviting about a quarter-mile away.

Propped up on a sofa, supported by pillows, was a strikingly handsome woman attended by Dr Fisher. She was middle-aged, with hair that had once been dark but now was heavily streaked with silver. Despite this, her vitality and commanding personality were unmistakable. Instantly, you sensed you were in the presence of a woman who, as the Irish say, possessed the power of the swell.

She acknowledged us with a graceful inclination of her head.

"Please sit, gentlemen."

We took our seats, and the magistrate's clerk positioned himself at a round table nearby.

"I trust, madam," Mr Andrews began gently, "it will not distress you too greatly to recount last night's events?"

"Not at all, sir. I fully understand how important it is to waste no time if those cowardly murderers are to be apprehended."

"Very good, madam. It may be easier if I pose questions directly, allowing you simply to answer. What time did you retire last night?"

"Half-past nine, sir. I was rather tired."

"And your husband?"

"About an hour later, I believe."

"Did he seem agitated or worried?"

"Not more than usual."

"What happened then?"

"We slept. Suddenly, I was awakened by a hand pressed tightly across my mouth. I tried to scream, but the hand prevented it. Two masked men were in the room."

"Could you describe them at all, madam?"

"One was very tall, with a long black beard. The other was short, stout, with a reddish beard. Both wore hats pulled down low, concealing their eyes."

"H'm!" murmured the magistrate thoughtfully. "I fear the beards were too prominent."

"You mean false beards?"

"Yes, madam. Please continue."

"The short man was restraining me. He forced a gag into my mouth and bound my hands and feet tightly with rope. The other stood beside my husband, holding my small dagger-like paper knife he'd taken from the dressing table, the blade pointing directly at Michael's heart. After the shorter man had bound me, he joined his companion, and together they forced my husband from bed and into the adjoining dressing room. I was close to fainting with fear, but I strained desperately to listen."

Her voice grew slightly stronger.

"They spoke too softly at first for me to catch their words clearly, but I recognised the language—a dialect of Spanish common in parts of Catalonia. They appeared to be demanding something from Michael, and soon their voices rose in anger. It was the tall man who spoke clearly first. 'You know what we want,' he said, 'the secret! Where is it?' I couldn't hear my husband's reply, but the other man shouted angrily, 'You lie! We know you have it. Where are your keys?'"

"Then I heard drawers being opened roughly. There is a safe in the dressing room wall, in which my husband kept a considerable amount of cash. Clare informed me it had indeed been forced open and robbed, though apparently it did not contain whatever they sought. Soon after, the taller man cursed angrily and ordered my husband to dress himself. Moments later, something seemed to disturb them—perhaps a noise in the clubhouse—for they rushed Michael back into my room, half-dressed."

"Pardon," Mulligan interrupted gently, "but is there no other exit from the dressing room?"

"No, sir, only the connecting door into our bedroom. They hurried Michael through, the shorter man leading and the taller one following, still holding the knife. Michael tried desperately to reach me. I saw the torment in his eyes. He turned back to the intruders. 'I must speak to her,' he pleaded. Then he quickly approached the bed. 'Everything will be all right, Saoirse,' he assured me. 'Don't be afraid. I'll return before morning.' But despite his attempt to sound confident, his eyes betrayed absolute terror. Immediately they dragged him out, the taller man warning fiercely, 'Make a sound—and you're a dead man!'"

"After that," Mrs Foley continued softly, "I must have fainted. My next memory is of Clare gently rubbing my wrists and giving me brandy."

"Mrs Foley," asked the magistrate, "do you have any idea what it was the assassins sought?"

"None whatsoever, sir."

"Were you aware that your husband feared any particular danger?"

"Yes. I had noticed a significant change in him."

"When was this?"

Mrs Foley thought carefully. "About ten days ago, perhaps."

"Not earlier?"

"It may have started earlier, but that's when I first noticed it clearly."

"Did you question your husband about his distress?"

"Once, but he answered evasively. Still, it was obvious he suffered some terrible anxiety. However, since he clearly wished to conceal it, I pretended to notice nothing."

"Did you know he'd summoned a detective?"

"A detective?" exclaimed Mrs Foley, astonished.

"Yes, this gentleman—Mr Rupert Mulligan." Mulligan bowed slightly. "He arrived today in response to a letter from your husband."

Taking Foley's letter from his pocket, Mulligan handed it to her. She read it with obvious shock.

"I had no knowledge of this. Clearly, he realised the extent of the danger."

"Madam," said the magistrate earnestly, "please be entirely frank. Can you recall any event in your husband's past in Spain that might explain his murder?"

Mrs Foley considered carefully before shaking her head.

"No, I cannot. My husband certainly had enemies—people he'd bested in business or otherwise—but I recall no specific incident. I don't deny there might be one, only that I'm unaware of it."

Mr Andrews stroked his beard uneasily.

"And you can pinpoint the exact time of this attack?"

"Yes. I distinctly recall the mantelpiece clock striking two."

She nodded toward a small travelling clock in a leather case resting on the mantelpiece. Mulligan rose, examined the clock closely, and nodded approvingly.

"And here's something else!" Blanchflower suddenly exclaimed. "A wristwatch—knocked from the dressing table by the intruders, no doubt, and smashed. Little did they realise it would provide evidence against them!"

Carefully, he removed the shards of glass, then suddenly stopped, looking utterly astonished.

"Mother Mary!" he gasped.

"What is it?"

"The watch hands—they point to seven o'clock!"

"Seven?" cried the examining magistrate incredulously.

But Mulligan, as quick as ever, gently took the broken watch from the startled inspector and pressed it to his ear. A faint smile appeared on his lips.

"The glass is broken, certainly, but the watch itself is still ticking."

This explanation was greeted with relieved smiles, but the magistrate soon raised another concern.

"Yet surely it is not seven o'clock now?"

"No," Mulligan replied calmly. "It is only a few minutes past five. Perhaps this watch gains somewhat, madam?"

Mrs. Foley looked slightly puzzled.

"It does gain," she admitted hesitantly. "But never so drastically as that."

With an impatient gesture, the magistrate dismissed the matter and resumed his questions.

"Madam, the front door was found ajar. It seems likely the assassins entered by it, yet it showed no sign of being forced. Can you offer an explanation?"

"Perhaps my husband took a final stroll outside and forgot to latch it upon returning."

"Would that have been typical behaviour?"

"Very. My husband was quite absent-minded."

A slight frown crossed her face as she spoke, indicating this particular trait in her husband may have occasionally troubled her.

"There is another inference we might draw," remarked the inspector suddenly. "Since the intruders insisted on Mr Foley dressing, it suggests the location to which they were taking him, where 'the secret' was hidden, lay some distance away."

The magistrate nodded thoughtfully.

"Yes, far enough away, yet still within reach, since Foley spoke of returning by morning."

"What time does the last train leave Magennis?" Mulligan asked abruptly.

"Eleven fifty in one direction, twelve seventeen in the other," answered Blanchflower. "But a waiting motorcar seems more probable."

"Of course," said Mulligan, looking slightly disappointed.

"Indeed," the magistrate continued more brightly, "that might give us a clue. A car carrying two foreigners would likely be remembered. Excellent point, Mr Blanchflower."

He nodded with satisfaction, then turned gravely back to Mrs. Foley.

"Another matter, madam. Do you know anyone by the name 'Corrigan'?"

"Corrigan?" she repeated thoughtfully. "No, not at present."

"You've never heard your husband mention that name?"

"Never."

"And do you know anyone whose first name is Abbie?"

He watched Mrs. Foley carefully, seeking any hint of recognition or discomfort, but she simply shook her head naturally.

The magistrate proceeded cautiously.

"Are you aware that your husband received a visitor last night?"

This time a slight colour rose to her cheeks, but she replied steadily:

"No. Who was it?"

"A lady."

"Indeed?"

The magistrate, however, did not press further. It seemed unlikely Madam Wiffen had any connection with the murder, and he wanted to spare Mrs. Foley unnecessary distress.

He signalled to the inspector, who promptly rose and walked across the room. He returned holding the glass jar we had earlier seen in the shed. From it, he took out the dagger.

"Madam," he said gently, "do you recognise this?"

She gave a sharp cry.

"Yes! That's my dagger." Then, noticing the stained blade, she recoiled, her eyes wide with horror. "Is that—blood?"

"Yes, madam. This weapon was used to murder your husband." He swiftly returned it to the jar. "You're certain this is the dagger that was on your dressing table last night?"

"Yes. It was a gift from my son, Terence. He was in the Army— drove tanks during the War, after lying about his age." Her voice held a touch of maternal pride. "The dagger is fashioned from tank armour wire, a wartime keepsake he gave me."

"I understand, madam. That leads us to another point. Where is your son now? We must contact him urgently."

"Terence? He's on his way to Lisbon."

"Lisbon?"

"Yes. My husband sent him to Belfast yesterday on business, but something occurred that required Terence to travel immediately to Spain. A ship left Belfast for Lisbon last night, and Michael telegraphed instructions for him to board it."

"Do you know anything about this business in Lisbon?"

"No, sir, only that Lisbon was not his final destination. From there, he was to travel overland to Barcelona."

In unison, both the magistrate and the inspector exclaimed: "Barcelona! Again Barcelona!"

At this moment, while we stood stunned by the repetition of that city's name, Mulligan suddenly approached Mrs. Foley. He had been standing by the window, seemingly lost in thought, and I wondered if he'd fully heard all that had transpired. He now bowed respectfully to her.

"Pardon me, madam, may I examine your wrists?"

Although slightly startled by the request, Mrs. Foley held out her wrists. Around each was a deep, cruel red mark from the tight cords. As Mulligan studied them, I thought I saw a brief flash of excitement in his eyes, but it faded immediately.

"They must cause you considerable pain," he remarked gently, once more looking uncertain.

The magistrate spoke urgently.

"Young Mr Foley must be contacted immediately by wireless. It's imperative we learn everything he knows about this journey to Barcelona." He hesitated briefly. "I had hoped he would be nearby, sparing you this ordeal, madam."

"You mean," she said softly, "the identification of my husband's body?"

The magistrate nodded solemnly.

"I am strong enough," she said firmly. "I can bear whatever is necessary. I am ready—now."

"Oh, tomorrow would be quite soon enough—" he began.

"I prefer to have it done," she said quietly, a brief shadow of pain crossing her face. "Doctor, if you will assist me?"

Dr. Fisher quickly stepped forward, wrapping a cloak around Mrs. Foley's shoulders, and we descended the staircase slowly.

Blanchflower hurried ahead to open the shed. Moments later Mrs. Foley stood in the doorway, pale but determined. She raised a hand to steady herself.

"A moment, gentlemen, while I brace myself."

She lowered her hand and gazed down at her husband. Then, the remarkable composure she had maintained collapsed entirely.

"Michael!" she cried in anguish. "My husband! Oh, dear God!" And, collapsing forward, she fell unconscious.

Mulligan was instantly at her side, quickly lifting an eyelid and checking her pulse. When he confirmed she'd genuinely fainted, he stepped back, pulling me aside.

"Lockhart, I am an utter fool! If there ever was genuine love and grief in a woman's voice, it was hers just now. My theory was entirely mistaken. Well! I must begin again!"

Chapter Six

Between them, the doctor and Mr Andrews carried the unconscious Mrs Foley into the clubhouse. Inspector Blanchflower watched them, shaking his head in sympathy.

"Poor woman," he murmured softly. "The shock has overwhelmed her. Well, there's nothing more we can do. Now, Mr Mulligan, shall we examine the actual scene of the crime?"

"If you please, Mr Blanchflower."

We passed through the clubhouse and out the front door. As we crossed the hall, Mulligan glanced at the staircase, shaking his head disapprovingly.

"It's unbelievable to me that the servants heard nothing. That staircase creaks loud enough, with three people descending, to awaken even the deepest sleeper!"

"It was the middle of the night, remember. They'd have been sound asleep."

But Mulligan continued shaking his head, clearly dissatisfied with that explanation. He paused on the drive, gazing thoughtfully at the clubhouse.

"What prompted them first to test whether the front door was unlocked? It was very improbable it would be. Surely, it would have been more logical to force a window first."

"But all the ground-floor windows are secured by iron shutters," objected the inspector.

Mulligan pointed upward to a first-floor window.

"That is the bedroom window we just left, is it not? Notice that tree—it would be remarkably easy to climb up there."

"Perhaps," admitted Blanchflower reluctantly, "but not without leaving clear footprints in the flower bed."

I recognised the truth of his remark. There were two large oval flower beds, bright with scarlet geraniums, flanking the steps up to the entrance. The tree Mulligan indicated grew from within the rear of one flower bed itself, making it impossible to reach without stepping directly onto the soft earth.

"You see," the inspector continued, "no footprints would appear on the paths or drive due to recent dry weather, but on the flower beds, the marks would be quite clear."

Mulligan stepped closer, carefully studying the flower bed. Indeed, as Blanchflower had described, the soil was smooth and undisturbed. Mulligan appeared to accept this, and we turned away—when suddenly he darted across to the other flower bed.

"Mr Blanchflower!" he called excitedly. "Look here. You have plenty of marks."

The inspector joined him, smiling indulgently.

"My dear Mr Mulligan, those are undoubtedly the gardener's footprints, made by heavy, hobnailed boots. And besides, they wouldn't help, since there's no tree on this side to give access to the upper storey."

"True," Mulligan conceded, looking distinctly deflated. "You're sure, then, these footprints mean nothing?"

"Absolutely they mean nothing," the inspector replied confidently.

Then, to my astonishment, Mulligan said firmly:

"I disagree entirely. In fact, I have a strong suspicion that these footprints are among the most significant clues we have yet uncovered."

Blanchflower merely shrugged, clearly suppressing his own scepticism.

"Shall we continue?" he asked, tactfully changing the subject.

"Certainly. I can investigate this footprint matter more fully later," Mulligan replied cheerfully.

Rather than returning down the main drive, Blanchflower guided us along a narrower path branching off at right angles. It curved upwards slightly, looping around the right side of the clubhouse, bordered on both sides by thick shrubbery. Abruptly, the path opened into a small clearing, from which we had a splendid view of the sea. A bench stood here, not far from a rather shabby outbuilding. A few steps further on, a neat row of bushes marked the boundary of the Royal County grounds. Blanchflower led us carefully through the bushes, and suddenly we stood on a broad stretch of open grassland. Looking around, I was astonished.

"Why, this golf course isn't even operational!" I exclaimed.

Blanchflower nodded calmly.

"The links are undergoing extensive refurbishment," he explained. "They're scheduled to open officially sometime next month. It was a few of the workmen engaged on this project who discovered Foley's body early this morning."

I gasped involuntarily. Slightly to my left, in a spot I hadn't initially noticed, was a long narrow excavation, and beside it, lying face-down, was a man's body! For a split second my heart jolted violently, as I imagined the tragedy had somehow repeated itself. But Inspector Blanchflower swiftly cleared my confusion, moving forward with an irritated exclamation:

"What on earth have my officers been doing? They were

explicitly instructed to prevent anyone approaching the scene without proper identification!"

The figure on the ground turned casually, glancing over his shoulder.

"But I have proper identification," he said calmly, slowly rising to his feet.

"My dear Mr Faulkner!" cried the inspector, startled. "I had no idea you'd arrived yet. The magistrate has been waiting impatiently for you."

As he spoke, I regarded the newcomer with intense curiosity. The renowned detective from the Belfast Royal Ulster Constabulary was familiar to me by reputation, and I eagerly studied him. He was a tall man of perhaps thirty, with copper-coloured hair and moustache, standing proudly erect in military fashion. His manner carried a certain arrogance, clearly reflecting his awareness of his own importance. Blanchflower introduced us, presenting Mulligan as a fellow investigator. At this, Detective Faulkner's eyes sparked briefly with interest.

"I know you by reputation, Mr Mulligan," Faulkner said abruptly. "You made quite a name for yourself in the old days, didn't you? But investigative methods have advanced greatly since then."

"Crimes, however, remain remarkably the same," Mulligan replied gently.

It was immediately clear to me that Faulkner intended to be antagonistic. He clearly resented Mulligan's presence and would, I sensed, withhold any significant clue he might discover.

"The examining magistrate—" Blanchflower tried to interject.

Faulkner cut him off rudely:

"Never mind the examining magistrate! It's the daylight that matters. We'll lose it completely within half an hour or so. I already know the basic facts, and the clubhouse occupants can wait until tomorrow. If we're to find any clues to the killers, this spot is our best hope. Are your officers responsible for trampling everywhere? I assumed they knew better nowadays."

"They certainly do. Those marks you're concerned about were made by the workmen who discovered the body."

Faulkner grunted in annoyance.

"Yes, the three sets of tracks clearly show where they came through the bushes—but they were cunning enough. You can just about distinguish Mr Foley's footprints in the centre, but the prints on either side have been carefully obliterated. Not that you'd see much anyway on ground as hard as this. Still, they weren't taking chances."

"You seek external clues," Mulligan remarked softly. "Physical evidence, correct?"

Faulkner stared at him impatiently.

"Obviously."

A faint, amused smile briefly appeared on Mulligan's lips. He seemed ready to say something but reconsidered. Instead, he stooped to examine a spade lying nearby.

"That's what they used to dig the grave, right enough," Faulkner commented dismissively. "But you won't get any clues from it. It's Foley's own spade, and whoever handled it wore gloves. See here," he indicated with his foot, "they left Foley's—or his gardener's—gloves behind, stained with soil. They weren't taking any risks, these killers. The victim stabbed with his own dagger, and to be buried using his own tools. They thought they'd leave no trace! But I'll outwit them. There's always some slip-up, and I intend to find it."

But Mulligan now seemed absorbed by another object—a short, discoloured length of lead piping lying near the spade. He prodded it lightly with one finger.

"And does this pipe also belong to the victim?" he inquired politely, with just a trace of irony.

Faulkner gave a careless shrug, plainly uninterested.

"It might have been here for weeks. Anyway, it doesn't concern me."

"I, on the contrary, find it extremely interesting," Mulligan replied pleasantly.

I suspected Mulligan was deliberately provoking the Belfast detective, and he succeeded admirably. Faulkner turned his back rudely, muttering about having no time to waste, and resumed closely examining the ground.

Meanwhile, Mulligan, appearing struck by a sudden thought, stepped back across the boundary to test the door of the little shed.

"That's locked," Faulkner called over his shoulder. "Just a gardener's storage shed for junk. The spade came from the proper toolshed near the clubhouse."

"Marvelous!" Blanchflower whispered to me in awed admiration. "He's only been here half an hour and already knows everything! What a remarkable fellow! Without question, Faulkner is today's greatest detective."

Although I found Faulkner disagreeable, I couldn't deny a grudging respect for his efficiency. The man radiated competence. I was privately dismayed that Mulligan had yet to achieve anything significant. In fact, he appeared focused on trivial, irrelevant details. Indeed, at precisely this moment he asked suddenly:

"Mr Blanchflower, please enlighten me—this whitewashed line encircling the grave, is it a police marking?"

"No, Mr Mulligan. That's connected with the golf course. It marks where a 'bunker,' as you call it, will be placed."

"A bunker?" Mulligan turned questioningly to me. "That's the irregular hole, usually filled with sand, having a bank on one side?"

I nodded in agreement.

"Mr Foley was fond of golf, I presume?"

"Yes, very keen indeed. It's mainly due to his influence and generous funding that the renovation of the golf course is proceeding. He even contributed to the design."

Mulligan nodded thoughtfully.

"Then they chose a rather poor spot to bury the body, didn't they? Almost as soon as the workers began digging, the murder would inevitably be discovered."

"Exactly!" Faulkner proclaimed triumphantly. "That proves the killers were unfamiliar with the place. It's excellent indirect evidence."

"Yes," Mulligan replied uncertainly. "No one acquainted with the golf course would choose such an obvious place to bury someone —unless they wished the body discovered. And that, naturally, would be absurd."

Faulkner didn't even bother replying.

"Yes," Mulligan continued, sounding oddly dissatisfied. "Yes— absurd indeed!"

Chapter Seven

As we retraced our steps toward the clubhouse, Mr Blanchflower excused himself, explaining that he needed to inform the examining magistrate immediately of Faulkner's arrival. Faulkner himself had appeared openly pleased when Mulligan announced he had seen all he needed. The last image we had, as we left the scene, was Faulkner crawling meticulously about on all fours, conducting a search whose thoroughness I could only admire. Mulligan, as if reading my mind, remarked ironically as soon as we were alone:

"So now you've met your ideal detective—the human bloodhound! Am I right, my friend?"

"At least he's doing something," I retorted sharply. "If there's anything to be found, he'll find it. Whereas you—"

"Well, I've also found something! A length of lead piping."

"Nonsense, Mulligan! You know perfectly well that has nothing to do with this case. I meant clues—small traces that might infallibly lead us to the murderers."

"My dear fellow, a clue two feet long is as valuable as one measuring two millimeters! It's merely a romantic notion that significant clues must always be tiny. As for the lead piping having nothing to do with the crime, you only think that because Faulkner says so. No"—he raised a hand as I began to protest—"let's say no more. Faulkner can pursue his methods, and I'll pursue mine. The case seems clear enough—yet, yet, my good friend, I'm not satisfied! And do you know why? Because of that wristwatch two hours ahead of time. Besides, several odd points remain unexplained. For instance, if revenge was the motive, why not simply stab Foley while he slept and be done with it?"

"They wanted the 'secret,' remember," I pointed out.

Mulligan absently flicked a speck of dust from his sleeve.

"Yes, but then—where is this 'secret'? Presumably at some distance, as they insisted he dress himself. Yet he's found murdered nearby, practically within earshot of the clubhouse. And again, isn't it rather coincidental that a weapon like the dagger was conveniently at hand?"

He paused, brow furrowing, before continuing:

"Why did the servants hear nothing? Were they drugged? Was there an accomplice who deliberately left the front door unlocked? I wonder if—"

He broke off abruptly, having reached the drive in front of the clubhouse. Suddenly, he turned decisively to me.

"My friend, I intend to astonish you—to please you! Your rebukes have touched me deeply. Let us examine some footprints!"

"Footprints? Where?"

"In the right-hand flower bed there. Mr Blanchflower insists they're merely the gardener's tracks. Let's verify if that's correct. See, here he approaches now, with his wheelbarrow."

Indeed, an elderly man was just crossing the drive, pushing a barrow loaded with seedlings. Mulligan called out, and the gardener promptly set down the barrow, hobbling over toward us.

"You mean to ask him for one of his boots, to compare with the footprints?" I asked excitedly, my faith in Mulligan reviving. Since he'd said the marks were important, presumably they were.

"Precisely," replied Mulligan.

"But won't he find that strange?"

"He won't think about it at all."

Further conversation was impossible as the gardener reached us.

"You wanted me for something, sir?"

"Yes. You have been gardener here for quite a long time, have you not?"

"Twenty-four years, sir."

"And your name is—?"

"Gerry, sir."

"I've been admiring your magnificent geraniums. Truly splendid. They must have been planted some time ago?"

"Yes indeed, sir. But naturally, to maintain the beds, one must regularly plant fresh seedlings, remove old ones, and keep spent blooms carefully picked."

"You planted some new seedlings yesterday, didn't you? Those in the middle there, and in the other bed as well?"

"Sir has sharp eyes! They always look a bit dull at first and take a day or two to perk up. Yes, I planted ten new seedlings in each bed last evening. As sir doubtless knows, planting should always be done out of the hot sun." Gerry was clearly delighted by Mulligan's interest and inclined to chat.

"That's a particularly fine specimen," Mulligan said, pointing at one. "Could I trouble you for a cutting of it?"

"Certainly, sir." Gerry promptly stepped into the flower bed, carefully cutting a slip from the plant Mulligan had admired.

Mulligan expressed his thanks effusively, and Gerry returned to his wheelbarrow.

"You see?" Mulligan smiled as he leaned down to examine the fresh indentation left by the gardener's hobnailed boot. "Quite simple."

"I didn't realize—"

"That the foot would be inside the boot? You don't use your mental faculties sufficiently, my friend. Well, what do you think of the footprint?"

I examined the bed closely.

"Every footprint in this bed was clearly made by the same boot," I finally said, after careful scrutiny.

"You think so? Good—I completely agree," Mulligan responded.

But he seemed distracted, his thoughts evidently elsewhere.

"Well," I remarked, "at least you can remove that bee from your bonnet now."

"Mother Mary! What a peculiar idiom! What exactly does it mean?"

"I meant you can finally give up your obsession with these footprints."

To my surprise, Mulligan shook his head emphatically.

"No, no, my friend. I've finally hit upon the correct track. I still lack illumination, but, as I hinted to Mr Blanchflower, these footprints are actually the most significant clue we've found so far. Poor Faulkner—I wouldn't be surprised if he ignored them entirely."

At that moment the clubhouse door opened, and Mr Andrews emerged with the inspector, descending the steps toward us.

"Ah, Mr Mulligan, we were just coming to find you," the

magistrate said briskly. "It grows late, but I wish to call upon Madam Wiffen. No doubt she'll be greatly distressed by Foley's murder, and we may learn something valuable from her. Perhaps the secret withheld from his wife was confided to the woman who had captured his heart. After all, we know where Samson's weakness lay, don't we?"

We said no more, but fell into step. Mulligan walked beside the examining magistrate, while the inspector and I followed a short distance behind.

"There's little doubt Rose's account was broadly accurate," Blanchflower remarked confidentially to me. "I made a quick call to headquarters. It appears Madam Wiffen has made three significant deposits into her bank account during the last six weeks—that is, since Foley arrived in Magennis. The total comes to two hundred thousand Irish pounds!"

"Good heavens," I mused, mentally calculating. "That must be nearly four thousand pounds!"

"Precisely. Yes, it's clear Foley was utterly infatuated. Still, whether or not he confided his secret to her remains to be seen. The magistrate is hopeful, though I'm less optimistic."

We had reached the lane, approaching the fork in the road where our car had stopped earlier. At that moment I realized Manor Carney, Madam Wiffen's residence, was the small house from which the beautiful girl had emerged.

"She has lived here many years," the inspector explained, nodding toward the house. "Quietly, unobtrusively. No known family or close friends other than local acquaintances. She never mentions the past or her husband—no one even knows whether he's alive or dead. There's a mystery about her, you understand."

My curiosity deepened. "And—the daughter?" I ventured cautiously.

"A beautiful young woman—modest, devout, everything one could wish. A girl to be pitied, really. Even if she knows nothing of her mother's past, a prospective husband would naturally make inquiries, and then—" The inspector shrugged cynically.

"But that wouldn't be her fault!" I protested indignantly.

"No. But what would you? Men are particular about a wife's origins."

Further conversation ended as we reached the house. Mr Andrews rang the bell. After a short pause, we heard footsteps approach, and the door slowly opened. There stood the young goddess from earlier that day. Upon seeing us, her face drained instantly of colour, leaving her deathly pale, eyes wide with apprehension. There could be no doubt—she was terrified!

"Madam Wiffen," said Mr Andrews, removing his hat with a flourish, "I am deeply sorry to intrude, but the demands of justice, you understand? Would you be so kind as to inform your mother that I request a few moments of her time?"

For a moment, the girl stood completely still. One hand rested against her side, as though trying to steady the sudden, overwhelming agitation within her. But she quickly regained her composure and spoke in a soft, controlled voice:

"I'll go and ask. Please, come in."

She stepped into a room just off the hall, and we caught the murmur of her voice as she announced our arrival. Then another voice replied—similar in tone, but carrying a firmer edge beneath its smoothness:

"Of course. Invite them in."

A minute later, we stood face to face with the enigmatic Madam Wiffen.

She was shorter than her daughter, her figure full and elegant with the poise of a woman in her prime. Her dark hair was parted in the centre and styled in the serene fashion of a Madonna. Half-lidded blue eyes regarded us with cool interest. She was no longer young, certainly, but her allure belonged to the sort that transcends age.

"You wished to speak with me, sir?" she asked calmly.

"Yes, madam," said Mr Andrews, clearing his throat. "We're in the process of investigating Mr Foley's death. You've heard of it, I presume?"

She inclined her head silently, her expression unchanging.

"We hoped you might be able to shed some light on the circumstances."

"Me?" Her tone held polite astonishment.

"Yes, madam. It's been suggested that you were in the habit of visiting Mr Foley at his home in the evenings. Is that accurate?"

A touch of colour rose in her pale cheeks, but her voice remained even.

"I don't believe you have the right to question me about that."

"Madam, this is a murder inquiry."

"Well then," she said sharply, "what of it? I had no part in any murder."

"We're not suggesting you did. But you knew the deceased well. Did he ever mention feeling endangered or threatened in any way?"

"No, never."

"Did he ever discuss his time in Barcelona or speak of enemies he made there?"

"No, he did not."

"Then you can't help us at all?"

"I'm afraid not. And frankly, I don't understand why you've come to me. Surely his wife is a better source for such matters?"

"Mrs Foley has shared all she knows."

"Ah," said Madam Wiffen, a faint trace of irony slipping into her voice. "I wonder—"

"You wonder what, madam?"

"Nothing," she said coolly.

Mr Andrews studied her closely. It was evident to him that this was a contest of wits—and his opponent was a formidable one.

"You maintain that Mr Foley never confided in you?"

"Why should he?" she replied smoothly. "Why do you suppose he would trust me with secrets?"

"Because, madam," said Mr Andrews, abandoning subtlety, "men often tell their mistresses what they do not confide to their wives."

At that, she recoiled as if struck. Her eyes blazed with fury.

"Sir, you insult me—before my daughter, no less! I've nothing to tell you. Kindly leave my house."

There was no mistaking it: she had won the exchange. We left Manor Carney like chastened schoolboys. Mr Andrews muttered irritably to himself, while Mulligan seemed lost in his own thoughts. Suddenly he snapped out of his reverie and turned to the magistrate.

"Is there a decent hotel nearby?" he asked.

"There's the Glenview Hotel, a modest place not far from here —on this side of town, a few hundred yards along the road. Convenient enough for your inquiries. Shall we expect to see you in the morning?"

"Yes, thank you, Mr Andrews."

After the usual polite farewells, the magistrate and inspector returned toward the golf course, while Mulligan and I strolled in the direction of Magennis.

"The Irish police system is truly remarkable," Mulligan remarked as we walked. "Their knowledge of people's affairs, right down to the most minor detail, is astonishing. Foley had been in Magennis little over six weeks, and yet they knew his habits thoroughly. And they seem just as informed about Madam Wiffen's banking activity—right down to the deposits she's made recently! The power of the dossier, my friend—never underestimate it."

Then he stopped abruptly, turning his head.

"What's that?"

A figure was racing toward us down the road, hair flying in the wind. It was Ciara Wiffen, hatless and breathless.

"Please forgive me," she gasped, reaching us. "I shouldn't be doing this—I know I shouldn't. Please don't tell my mother. But —is it true? What people are saying, that Mr Foley called in a detective before he died? And... you are he?"

"Yes, miss," said Mulligan gently. "It's quite true. But how did you hear of it?"

"Rose told our Maureen," she explained with a bashful blush.

Mulligan pulled a face. "So much for secrecy! But then again, it scarcely matters. What is it you wish to know?"

The girl hesitated. She clearly wanted to speak, but fear held her back. Finally, she whispered:

"Is—anyone suspected?"

Mulligan studied her intently.

"Suspicion is in the air, miss," he said carefully.

"Yes, I know. But is there—anyone specific?"

"Why do you ask?"

She flinched slightly at the question. Then, after a pause, she said:

"Mr Foley was always very kind to me. Naturally I'm concerned."

"I understand," said Mulligan. "Well then, at present suspicion centres around two individuals."

"Two?" she echoed, and though it was subtle, I was certain I heard both surprise—and relief—in her voice.

"Yes. We don't yet know their names, but we believe they are Catalonians—from Barcelona. And there you have it, miss. You see what comes of youth and beauty—I've let professional secrets slip!"

She laughed lightly, then thanked him shyly.

"I'd best go now. Mother will be wondering where I am."

With that, she turned and ran back up the road, as graceful as a nymph. I watched her go, spellbound.

"My good sir," Mulligan said with amused irony, "are we to remain rooted here all night, simply because you've seen a pretty girl and your senses have deserted you?"

I laughed, a little sheepishly.

"She is beautiful, Mulligan. Who wouldn't be dazzled?"

But to my surprise, Mulligan shook his head solemnly.

"Ah, my dear friend, do not fall for Ciara Wiffen. She is not for you. Trust Papa Mulligan on that."

"Why? The inspector swore she was as good as she is beautiful. An angel!"

"Some of the worst criminals I've known had angelic faces," Mulligan replied cheerfully. "It's not uncommon for a flawed brain to sit beneath the visage of a saint."

"Mulligan!" I cried, horrified. "Surely you don't suspect that innocent girl?"

"Tut-tut! Calm yourself. I didn't say I suspected her. But you must admit, her eagerness to learn about the investigation is... unusual."

"You're wrong," I said firmly. "Her concern isn't for herself—it's for her mother."

"My friend," said Mulligan dryly, "as always, you see nothing. Madam Wiffen is more than capable of looking after herself. Her daughter has no need to worry on that front. I admit, I was teasing you earlier—but I meant what I said. Don't set your heart on that girl. She's not for you. I, Rupert Mulligan, know it."

He fell silent for a moment, then added thoughtfully:

"Dash it all—I just can't recall where I've seen that face before."

"Ciara's?" I asked.

"No, her mother's."

I stared at him.

"Yes," he continued. "It was years ago, back when I was still with the police in England. I never met her in person, but I definitely saw her photograph—connected to a case. I believe it may have been..."

"Yes?"

"A murder case," said Mulligan grimly.

Chapter Eight

We arrived at the clubhouse quite early the next morning. The guard at the gate made no attempt to stop us this time; instead, he offered a respectful salute as we passed through to the front entrance. Just as we stepped inside, we saw Clare descending the stairs—evidently not averse to pausing for a bit of conversation.

Mulligan inquired politely about Mrs Foley's condition.

Clare shook her head sadly.
"She's heartbroken, poor soul. She won't touch a bite to eat—not a morsel! Pale as a ghost, she is. It's painful to watch. I tell you this, sir—not for all the world would I waste my grief on a man who'd wronged me with another woman!"

Mulligan nodded sympathetically.
"What you say is quite fair. But alas, the heart of a woman in love will forgive far more than reason allows. Still, surely there must have been some quarrels between them these past few months?"

But Clare shook her head again, with certainty.
"Never once! I never heard madam say a harsh word—or even a word of reproach. She was an angel by temperament. Sir, though —he was very different."

"Mr Foley lacked the temper of a saint?" asked Mulligan mildly.

"Quite the opposite. When he lost his temper, the whole house would know! The day he had it out with Mr Terence—you'd think the shouting reached all the way to Ballyroney! No holding back between them, I tell you."

"Really?" said Mulligan, with interest. "When did this altercation take place?"

"Just before Mr Terence left for Belfast. He nearly missed his train. I saw him dash out of the library and grab his bag from the hall. The car was being fixed that day, so he had to run to the station. I was dusting the salon as he passed—and his face was white as paper, except for two blazing red patches. He was fuming!"

Clare was clearly relishing the retelling.

"And the quarrel—what was it about?" asked Mulligan.

"That, I couldn't tell you," admitted Clare. "They were shouting so loudly and so fast, and the accents from their part of the country are so thick—you'd need to have grown up there to understand a word of it! But all day after, sir was like a thundercloud—nothing pleased him!"

A door slammed upstairs, cutting short her chatter.

"And Rose is waiting on me!" Clare exclaimed, suddenly recalling her responsibilities. "She'll scold me proper, that one!"

"One moment more, please. Do you know where the examining magistrate is?"

"They're out back, looking over the automobile in the garage. The inspector suspects it might've been used the night of the murder."

"Quite a logical supposition," murmured Mulligan, as Clare bustled away.

"You're going to join them, then?" I asked.

"No, I'll wait for their return in the salon. It's cool in there—and this morning is sweltering."

This leisurely attitude didn't sit well with me.

"If you don't mind," I said, hesitating.

"Not at all. You wish to do a little sleuthing of your own?"

"Well, I thought I might find Faulkner and see what he's up to."

"The human foxhound," Mulligan murmured, settling into a chair and closing his eyes. "By all means, my friend. Go sniff around."

I stepped out the front door into the rising heat. Instead of heading straight for the crime scene, I turned into the shrubbery off to the right, intending to come out onto the links a little further down from where we'd emerged yesterday. The undergrowth here was much thicker, and I had quite a battle pushing through. I burst out onto the golf course so abruptly that I collided full force with a young woman standing with her back to the thicket.

She let out a startled gasp, and I, too, recoiled in shock—because it was Belle, my lively companion from the train.

The recognition was mutual.

"You!" we both cried in unison.

Belle recovered her poise first.

"My only aunt! What are you doing here?" she exclaimed.

"More to the point—what are you doing here?" I retorted.

"Last I saw you, you were dutifully on your way back to London."

"And the last I saw of you," I reminded her, "you were heading off with your sister like a proper little girl. How *is* your sister, by the way?"

That earned me a bright flash of teeth.

"So kind of you to ask! My sister is very well, thank you."

"She's here with you, I presume?"

"She stayed behind in town," said Belle with a mock-serious air.

"I don't believe you have a sister at all," I laughed. "And if you do, her name is probably Harris!"

"Do you at least remember *my* name?" she asked, slyly.

"Belle. But I'm expecting you to give me the real one this time."

She shook her head mischievously.
"Not a chance."

"Not even a hint as to why *you're* here?"

"Oh, that's easy. Ever heard of actors 'resting' between engagements?"

"At luxury Irish resorts?"

"It's all dirt cheap if you know the right places," she said smugly.

I studied her closely.
"Still, you had no plan to come here when I saw you two days ago."

"We all face disappointments," she replied philosophically. "And now I've said quite enough. Little boys shouldn't be so nosy. You haven't told me what *you're* doing here yet."

"You remember my friend, the detective?"

"Yes?"

"Well, perhaps you've heard about the murder—at the County Golf Course?"

Her expression changed instantly. Her breath caught and her eyes widened.

"You're mixed up in *that*?" she breathed.

I nodded. For once, I held the upper hand. The effect on her was gratifying. For several moments she just stared, stunned. Then she nodded energetically.

"Well, if that doesn't take the biscuit! Come on, I want to see all the horrors!"

"What do you mean?"

"Exactly what I said. Didn't I tell you I'm mad about crimes? I've been nosing around all morning. And now—bingo! I bump into you. Show me everything—the murder spot, the weapon, any juicy fingerprints you've got lying about."

"But look here—I can't! The place is off limits. They're being *very* strict."

"Aren't you one of the top brass now?"

I hesitated. My ego wasn't eager to give up the role.

"Why are you so keen?" I asked. "What do you expect to find?"

"Oh, everything. I've never had the chance to be in the thick of a real murder before. It'll be something to remember for life!"

Her morbid enthusiasm repulsed me.

"I'm sorry," I said stiffly. "But this isn't entertainment. It's a serious matter."

"Oh, get off your high horse," she retorted. "Don't act so superior. When *you* got called into this, did you turn up your nose and say, 'Oh no, what a dreadful business, I shan't be involved'?"

"No, but—"

"And if you'd been here on holiday and *not* involved, you'd have been poking your nose around like the rest of us. Admit it."

"I'm a man. You're a woman," I protested lamely.

"Your idea of a woman," Belle said, "is someone who jumps on a chair and screams when she sees a mouse. That's ancient history. But you *will* show me around, won't you? You see, it might be really important to me."

"How so?"

"They're keeping all the journalists out. But if I could get a scoop —something none of the papers have yet—it could make a huge difference. You've no idea what they'll pay for an exclusive."

I hesitated. That's when she slid her hand into mine—soft, warm, and persuasive.

"Please—be a darling."

I gave in. Truthfully, the idea of playing tour guide held a certain appeal.

We started at the place where the body had been found. A guard was stationed there, but he recognised me and offered a salute, raising no objection to my companion. Presumably, he assumed she was with me in some official capacity. I explained how the body had been discovered, and Belle listened attentively, occasionally asking questions—some of them surprisingly insightful.

From there, we headed toward the manor. I moved with caution; the last thing I wanted was to run into anyone. Taking her around the back through the shrubbery, I led her to the shed where the body had been temporarily stored. I remembered that the evening before, after relocking the door, Mr Blanchflower had handed the key to McGrady—the Ulster officer stationed outside the salon—"in case Mr Faulkner needed it while we're upstairs." I figured it was still with him.

Leaving Belle hidden from sight in the undergrowth, I slipped inside the clubhouse. McGrady stood as before outside the salon. From within, I could hear the low murmur of voices.

"You're looking for Mr Andrews? He's in there, speaking with Rose again."

"No, not exactly," I said quickly. "But I'd be very grateful if I could borrow the key to the shed outside. That is—if it's permitted."

"Of course, sir." He handed it over readily. "Mr Andrews instructed that you be given every assistance. Just return it to me when you're done."

"I will," I promised.

That small act of trust lifted my spirits. Clearly, in McGrady's eyes at least, I carried some of Mulligan's authority.

Belle was waiting just where I'd left her, eyes sparkling with anticipation.

"You got it?"

"Obviously," I replied with calm assurance. "Though strictly speaking, what we're doing is very much against the rules."

"You're a dear. I won't forget it. Let's go—no one from the clubhouse can see us, can they?"

"Just a moment," I said, stopping her. "I'm not going to stop you if you're determined to go in. But are you *sure* you want to? You've seen the grave, heard the story. Isn't that enough? This next bit is going to be... unpleasant."

She looked at me oddly, as though something deeper stirred behind her bright facade. Then she laughed lightly.

"I live for the gruesome, remember? Let's get on with it."

We reached the shed. I unlocked the door and we stepped inside. I crossed to where the body lay, and gently pulled back the sheet, just as Blanchflower had done the previous day. Belle let out a soft gasp, and I turned to see her face. The bravado had vanished. Her cheerful energy had drained away, replaced by a stark, almost frozen look of horror.

She hadn't taken my warning seriously, and now she was paying the price. I felt little sympathy. If she'd come this far out of morbid curiosity, then let her see it through.

I turned the body over with care.

"There—you see," I said. "He was stabbed in the back."

Her voice was barely a whisper.

"With what?"

I gestured toward the glass jar on the shelf.

"That dagger."

Suddenly she swayed, then collapsed in a heap. I rushed to her side.

"You're faint. Come out of here. This has been too much."

"Water," she breathed. "Quickly. Water."

I left her where she lay and dashed back to the clubhouse. Luckily, the halls were empty, and I managed to get a glass of water and discreetly add a splash from my hip flask. When I returned, Belle hadn't moved. I held the glass to her lips, and a few sips revived her almost instantly.

"Get me out of here—please," she gasped, trembling.

I supported her with my arm and guided her out into the sunshine. She pulled the shed door shut behind us and took a long, steadying breath.

"That's better. Oh, it was ghastly! Why did you let me go in there?"

I couldn't help but smile. It was such a classic response—quintessentially feminine. Strangely, I was comforted by her collapse. It reassured me that she wasn't as callous as I'd feared. For all her brashness, she was just a curious, overconfident girl who hadn't thought things through.

"I *did* try to stop you," I reminded her gently.

"Yes, I suppose you did. Well—goodbye."

"You can't just walk off on your own. You're still pale. I insist on walking you back to town."

"Nonsense, I'm fine now."

"What if you faint again? I insist."

She argued the point, but in the end, I prevailed. She let me walk with her as far as the edge of Magennis. We retraced our earlier route, passing the burial site, then taking a side path toward the road. When the first few shops came into view, she paused and turned to me.

"Well, this is where we part ways. Thank you—for everything."

"You're certain you're all right?"

"Perfectly. And I hope you won't get into any trouble for what you've shown me."

I waved the thought away.

"Well then—goodbye."

"*Slán go fóill,*" I said, smiling. "If you're staying in town, I'm sure we'll meet again."

She returned my smile.

"I like that. *Slán go fóill*, then."

"Wait—what's your address?"

"Oh, I'm staying at the Cherryhill Hotel. It's small but nice. Come visit me tomorrow."

"I will," I said with more enthusiasm than perhaps was necessary.

I watched her disappear down the road, then turned back toward the manor. I realized with a start that I hadn't locked the shed. Thankfully, no one seemed to have noticed. I returned the key to McGrady, and as I handed it over, a thought struck me:

Belle had told me where she was staying...
But I still didn't know her last name.

Chapter Nine

When I entered the salon, the examining magistrate was in the midst of questioning old Gerry, the gardener. Mulligan greeted me with a faint smile, and the inspector inclined his head politely. I slipped into a chair and listened in.

Mr Andrews, diligent and exacting as always, pressed on with his questioning—but gained very little of real use.

The gardening gloves? Yes, they were Gerry's. He wore them when handling a certain type of primula, which could cause a rash in some people. He couldn't recall when he'd last used them, and no, he hadn't missed them. As for storage, they were kept here and there—wherever he happened to toss them. The spade in question? Normally stored in the small tool shed, which, he affirmed, was kept locked. The key? It was left in the door. There was nothing worth stealing, after all—no reason to suspect burglars or assassins. Things like this didn't happen in Lord Wallace's time, he grumbled.

Mr Andrews indicated he was done, and the old man left, still muttering under his breath.

Remembering Mulligan's odd fixation with the footprints in the flower beds, I studied Gerry closely as he gave his answers. Either he was completely innocent—or an actor of rare talent.

Just as he reached the door, a thought struck me.

"Mr Andrews, pardon me—may I ask the witness one question?"

"By all means," said the magistrate, gesturing encouragingly.

I turned to Gerry. "Where do you usually keep your boots?"

"On my feet," he growled. "Where else would I keep them?"

"But at night—when you go to bed?"

"Under the bed."

"And who cleans them?"

"Clean them?" He let out a scornful laugh. "Why would anyone bother? I don't parade myself like a young dandy. I've got Sunday boots for Sunday, but otherwise—" He shrugged again.

I sat back, disappointed.

"Well," Mr Andrews said, "we're not exactly making great strides. It seems we'll have to wait for the cable from Barcelona. Has anyone seen Faulkner, by the way? That fellow has no manners at all. I'm half-inclined to send someone after him—"

"You won't have to look far."

The voice, calm and quiet, came from the open window. We all turned in surprise to see Faulkner standing there, one hand resting on the sill.

With a light movement, he stepped through the window and into the room.

"Here I am, gentlemen. My apologies for not appearing sooner."

"No matter, no matter," said Mr Andrews, a little flustered.

"Of course," Faulkner continued smoothly, "I'm merely a detective—not familiar with the intricacies of formal questioning. Still, if I were conducting one, I'd close the windows. After all, anyone standing outside can hear everything being said. But never mind."

Mr Andrews reddened slightly. Clearly, there was no love lost between the magistrate and the detective. Faulkner's arrogance grated on Andrews, who took his position very seriously. To Faulkner, magistrates were an obstruction—fussy bureaucrats with no real grasp of criminal investigation.

"Well, Mr Faulkner," Andrews said testily. "I trust you've used your time marvellously. Have you come to deliver the names of the assassins and their current location?"

The sarcasm rolled off Faulkner without effect.

"I've at least discovered where they came from."

He reached into his pocket and produced two small items, laying them on the table. We gathered around. A cigarette end and an unlit match.

Faulkner turned to Mulligan with a sharp look.

"What do you see?"

The tone was unnecessarily curt, and my cheeks flushed with indignation. But Mulligan, unbothered, merely lifted his shoulders in a slight shrug.

"A cigarette stub and a match."

"And what do they tell you?"

"They tell me nothing."

"Aha!" Faulkner smiled with smug satisfaction. "You haven't studied this sort of detail. That match—while unremarkable to you—isn't made in Ireland. It's common in Spain. Luckily it wasn't used, or I might not have recognised it. My guess is, one of the men dropped it while lighting a new cigarette."

"And the match he *did* use?" Mulligan asked quietly. "You found that as well?"

"No."

"Then perhaps your search wasn't as thorough as you believe."

For a moment Faulkner bristled, clearly stung. But he recovered quickly.

"You enjoy your little jests, Mr Mulligan. Regardless, this match is enough. As is the cigarette stub. It's a Spanish brand, wrapped in liquorice-pulp paper."

Mulligan bowed, and the inspector interjected.

"Couldn't they have belonged to Mr Foley? He *did* return from Spain only two years ago."

"No," Faulkner replied confidently. "I've already examined his personal effects. He used a different brand of cigarette and completely different matches."

"And yet," Mulligan said softly, "you don't find it strange that these men arrived unarmed, without gloves or a spade—and just happened to find everything they needed lying about?"

Faulkner gave him a thin smile.

"It would seem strange—unless you accept the theory I'm working on."

"Ah," said Mr Andrews, leaning forward. "And that theory is?"

"That they had help—from someone within the house."

"Or someone from outside it," Faulkner added cryptically.

"But surely someone must have *let* them in?" Mr Andrews protested. "It can't have been sheer luck that they found the front door unlatched!"

Faulkner didn't answer immediately. Instead, he simply smiled again—and to my mind, it was not a pleasant smile at all.

"The door was opened for them," Faulkner said, "but it could just as easily have been opened from the outside—by someone with a key."

"And who would have had such a key?" the magistrate asked.

Faulkner gave a careless shrug.
"Whoever had one certainly isn't going to admit it. But think about it—there are several possible candidates. Mr Terence Foley, for instance. He's on his way to Spain now, true, but perhaps he lost his key... or someone took it. Then there's the gardener—he's been here for years. One of the maids might have a sweetheart. It's easy enough to get an impression made and have a duplicate key cut. Plenty of possibilities. And then there's one person who, I think, is very likely to have one."

"And who might that be?" asked Mr Andrews.

"Madam Wiffen," Faulkner said.

"Ah!" Andrews exclaimed. "So you've heard about *that*, have you?"

Faulkner's tone was mild. "I hear everything."

"Well then, let me surprise you for once." Andrews leaned forward, clearly pleased to be the one holding the upper hand. He recounted the tale of the mysterious female visitor from the night of the murder. He mentioned the cheque fragment made out to 'Corrigan', and finally produced the letter signed by 'Abbie'.

Faulkner examined the items with interest. "Fascinating. But nothing that alters my theory."

"And what exactly *is* your theory?" the magistrate prompted.

"For now, I'll keep it to myself. I've only just begun to dig into this."

"Tell me one thing," Mulligan said suddenly. "Your theory explains how the door was opened. But what about why it was left open afterward? Surely it would've made sense to close it—otherwise, a patrol officer might have seen it ajar and raised an alarm."

"Bah. They made a mistake. It slipped their minds."

But Mulligan shook his head. "No. It wasn't an oversight. The open door was deliberate—or necessary. Any theory that ignores that detail is doomed to failure."

We all looked at Mulligan, taken aback. I had expected him to still be stinging from Faulkner's earlier one-upmanship about the match and cigarette end. But he seemed entirely at ease, even smug, as he spoke.

Faulkner twirled his moustache and shot him a mocking look. "You don't agree with me, eh? Then what *does* strike you about this case? Let's hear *your* take."

"There's something familiar about it," Mulligan replied. "Tell me, doesn't this whole affair remind you of another case?"

Faulkner frowned. "No. Should it?"

"You're mistaken. A remarkably similar crime has occurred before."

"Where? When?"

"That," Mulligan said regretfully, "I can't recall just yet. But I will. I'd hoped you might be able to help me place it."

Faulkner let out a sceptical snort.
"There've been lots of incidents involving masked men. They all blur together. Crimes tend to look the same."

"Ah," Mulligan replied, sliding seamlessly into lecture mode. "But that's where the psychology of crime comes in. As Mr Faulkner knows, criminals often develop habits—methods they return to. Just like the police, who can often identify a criminal by the way he operates. Isn't that right, Lockhart? Wood would agree with me, too."

He looked around the room, his tone measured but firm.

"People aren't imaginative. They repeat themselves. The respectable man and the criminal both follow patterns. Take the Englishman who killed his wives in bathtubs—had he switched things up, he might never have been caught. But he didn't. He followed the same routine. That's what gave him away."

"And your point?" Faulkner asked, unimpressed.

"My point," said Mulligan, "is that when you see two crimes committed with the same technique, you're likely looking at the same person. That's what I'm hunting—a familiar mind. You may know cigarettes, Mr Faulkner, but I know the human brain."

Faulkner didn't respond. His face was a blank wall.

"And here's another little tidbit you may not have heard yet," Mulligan added. "Mrs. Foley's wristwatch? It was found to be two hours fast the day after the murder."

Faulkner blinked. "Perhaps it's just fast naturally?"

"As it happens, yes," Mulligan admitted. "But even so—two hours? That's quite a lot."

"And those footprints in the flower bed," he added, nodding towards the open window.

Faulkner moved instantly, taking two steps to peer out. "I don't see any footprints."

"No," said Mulligan with perfect calm, rearranging a stack of books on a nearby table. "There are none."

For a brief second, Faulkner's face darkened. Rage flared across his features, and he stormed two steps toward Mulligan with clenched fists—until the salon door swung open and McGrady entered with an announcement.

"Mr Hall, the secretary, has just arrived from England. May he come in?"

Chapter Ten

The man who entered was instantly commanding. Tall and powerfully built, with the bronzed face and neck of someone long accustomed to the sun, he radiated confidence. Even Faulkner seemed pallid beside him. Later, I would come to appreciate that Philip Hall was no ordinary man. English by birth, he had led a life of adventure—hunting big game in Africa, trading in Persia, ranching in Texas, and wandering the islands of the Dutch East Indies.

His keen gaze found Mr Andrews at once.

"You're the examining magistrate in charge? Pleased to meet you, sir. What a ghastly business this is. How's Mrs. Foley holding up? It must've been a terrible shock."

"Truly dreadful," Mr Andrews replied gravely. "Let me introduce District Inspector Blanchflower, Mr Faulkner from the Royal Ulster Constabulary, Mr Rupert Mulligan—whom Mr Foley summoned, though unfortunately too late to prevent this tragedy—and Captain Lockhart, a friend of Mr Mulligan's."

Hall gave Mulligan a long, assessing look. "So Foley sent for you?"

"You weren't aware he intended to call in a detective?" Blanchflower asked.

"No," Hall said. "But I can't say I'm surprised."

"Oh?" Andrews prompted. "And why not?"

"Because the old man was on edge. I couldn't say what it was about—he never opened up to me—but he was definitely rattled."

"H'm," said the magistrate thoughtfully. "You have no idea what might've caused it?"

"No, sir. I don't."

"I hope you'll pardon a few routine questions. Your full name?"

"Philip Hall."

"How long have you been Mr Foley's secretary?"

"About two years. I met him through a mutual friend when he'd just come back from Spain. He offered me the post, and I took it. He was a first-rate employer."

"Did he speak much about his time in Spain?"

"Yes, now and then."

"Did he ever mention being in Barcelona?"

"Oh yes, several times."

"Anything specific? A particular incident that might've led to a vendetta or enemies?"

"Not that I recall."

"Did he ever speak of having some kind of secret?"

"Not that I can remember. But there was definitely a mystery about him. He never mentioned his early life—not a word about his childhood or time in Australia, where he was born. He was tight-lipped when he chose to be."

"So, as far as you know, he had no enemies? No secret someone might kill him to obtain?"

"That's right."

"Have you ever heard the name 'Corrigan' mentioned in connection with Mr Foley?"

Hall frowned, repeating the name under his breath. "Corrigan... It rings a bell, but I can't place it."

"What about a woman named Abbie? A friend of Mr Foley's?"

Again, Hall shook his head. "Abbie Corrigan? That's the full name? Strange... it's familiar, but I can't remember from where."

Mr Andrews cleared his throat.

"You understand, Mr Hall, this case demands complete transparency. We were just saying—hypothetically, of course—that someone in your position might feel inclined to protect Mrs. Foley, for whom I gather you have a great regard. But I must stress—no withholding of information."

Hall looked at him squarely, eyes widening in mild surprise.

"I don't follow. What does Mrs. Foley have to do with anything? I've got all the respect in the world for her, but I can't see how she fits in."

"No?" said Andrews, watching him closely. "Even if this 'Abbie Corrigan' was something more than just a friend to her husband?"

"Ah," said Hall slowly. "I see what you're driving at. But I'll bet anything you like—you're dead wrong. Foley wasn't that kind of man. He adored his wife. They were devoted, through and through."

Andrews shook his head, his tone more delicate now.

"We have a love letter, Mr Hall. Written by this Abbie. It accuses Mr Foley of neglecting her... of turning cold. That's not all. We also have evidence that he was conducting a liaison with a local woman, Madam Wiffen, who lives at the neighbouring manor."

Hall's expression sharpened.

"With all due respect, sir, that doesn't wash. I knew Foley. What you're suggesting just doesn't add up. There must be another explanation."

"And what would that be?" asked Andrews skeptically.

"What makes you so sure it was a romantic affair?"

"Well," said Andrews, "Madam Wiffen visited him frequently in the evenings. And since Mr Foley arrived in Magennis, she's been making large cash deposits—four thousand English pounds, to be exact."

Hall didn't flinch. "Yes, that's right. I arranged those payments for him. All in notes, at his request. But I'll tell you something— it wasn't romance."

"No? Then what was it?"

Hall leaned forward and smacked the table with his palm.

"Blackmail," he said sharply. "That's what it was."

There was a collective intake of breath.

"Blackmail?" Andrews repeated, clearly rattled.

"You heard me," Hall said. "Foley was being bled dry—and fast. Four thousand pounds in a couple of months? That's no love affair. That's extortion. I told you there was a mystery in Foley's past—and evidently this Madam Wiffen had the goods on him."

The inspector looked excited. "It's plausible. Definitely plausible."

"Possible?" Hall thundered. "It's a certainty. Tell me, have you put this love affair nonsense to Mrs. Foley?"

"No, sir," said Mr Andrews with some stiffness. "We wished to spare her any unnecessary distress."

"Distress? She'd laugh in your face. I tell you, she and Foley were a rare pair—devoted like few others."

"That brings me to another point," said the magistrate. "Were you ever made aware of the provisions in Mr. Foley's will?"

"I was. In fact, I took the will to the solicitors myself after he drew it up. If you want, I can give you their names. It was straightforward: half in trust to his wife for her lifetime, the other half to his son, with a few small legacies. I believe I was left a thousand."

"And when was this drawn up?"

"Oh, about eighteen months ago."

"Then it may surprise you to learn that another will was made less than a fortnight ago."

Hall blinked. "I had no idea. What did it say?"

"The entirety of his fortune was left outright to his wife. No mention of his son at all."

Hall let out a low whistle. "That's a tough blow for the boy. His mother dotes on him, of course, but to the outside world it looks like a lack of trust—or worse. That'll hurt. Still, it proves what I said before—Foley and his wife were solid."

"Indeed," said Mr Andrews, nodding. "It appears we may need to reassess some of our assumptions. We've cabled Barcelona, and once we receive their reply, all may become clear. That said, if your theory of blackmail is correct, then Madam Wiffen may be more useful than we'd imagined."

Mulligan spoke up suddenly. "Mr Hall, about the chauffeur—Masters. Had he been with Mr Foley long?"

"Over a year."

"Do you happen to know if he'd ever been in Spain?"

"I'm certain he hasn't. Before Foley, he worked for a family I know well in Gloucestershire. Never left the country as far as I know."

"So he's above suspicion?"

"Completely."

Mulligan looked mildly disappointed, but said nothing more.

Just then, the magistrate summoned McGrady.

"My compliments to Madam Foley," he said. "I should be grateful if she would permit me a few moments' conversation. Please assure her that I'll come to her—there's no need for her to trouble herself."

McGrady saluted and departed. But only a few minutes had passed when, to our collective surprise, the door opened and Mrs. Foley entered the room herself.

She was pale, dressed in heavy mourning, and walked with a quiet dignity. Mr Andrews jumped to his feet and hurried forward with concern, offering a chair and exclaiming apologies. She thanked him with a faint smile. Hall stepped forward, taking her hand with visible compassion, his expression deeply moved.

Mrs. Foley turned to the magistrate. "You wished to speak with me?"

"If you are willing, madam. I understand your husband was Irish-Australian. Can you tell me anything about his early life?"

She shook her head.

"He rarely spoke of it. I believe he came from the North-West, but I've always thought his childhood must have been unhappy. He avoided the subject completely. Our lives were focused on the present and what was ahead of us."

"Was there anything unusual—any mystery—in his past?"

Mrs. Foley gave a faint, ironic smile. "I'm afraid it's not so romantic as that, sir."

Mr Andrews smiled in return. "Quite so—we mustn't turn everything into melodrama." He hesitated. "There is, however, one more matter..."

But Hall interrupted, speaking quickly and with obvious annoyance.

"They've got a wild notion, Mrs. Foley. Apparently they believe Foley was having an affair with a woman next door—this Madam Wiffen."

Instantly, a flush of colour rose in Mrs. Foley's cheeks. Her head snapped up, but she bit her lip as her face trembled. Hall stared at her, astonished. Then Blanchflower leaned forward, speaking with unusual gentleness.

"We don't wish to upset you, madam. But is there any reason to think that Madam Wiffen may indeed have been involved with your husband?"

Mrs. Foley gave a sob, hiding her face in her hands. Her shoulders shook. When she finally looked up, her voice was low and unsteady.

"She may have been."

A stunned silence followed her admission. I had never seen anyone so visibly shocked as Hall. He stood frozen, completely unprepared for the revelation.

Chapter Eleven

I can't say what direction the conversation might have taken next, because at that very moment, the door flew open with force and a tall young man strode into the room.

For an instant, I had the eerie impression that the dead man had returned to life. But then I noticed the newcomer's hair was dark and free of grey, and I realised that this was just a youth—a mere boy—who had entered so abruptly. Without the slightest regard for those present, he rushed straight to Mrs. Foley.

"Mother!"

"Terence!" she cried, gathering him into her arms. "My darling! But what on earth are you doing here? You were supposed to have sailed on the *Esperanza* from Belfast two days ago!" She then seemed to remember the rest of us, and with a composed grace turned to introduce him: "My son, gentlemen."

"Ah!" said Mr Andrews, nodding in response to the young man's brief bow. "So you did not depart on the *Esperanza* as scheduled?"

"No, sir. As I was about to explain, the *Esperanza* was delayed twenty-four hours due to engine trouble. I should have departed last night instead of the night before, but I happened to pick up an evening paper—and there I saw the report about the—about the terrible tragedy that has happened—" His voice cracked, and his eyes welled with tears. "My poor father—my poor, poor father."

Mrs. Foley looked at him as if in a trance. "So you didn't sail?" she echoed, then added, more to herself than anyone else, with a weary motion of her hand, "It makes no difference now."

"Please sit down, Mr Foley," said Mr Andrews, gesturing toward a chair. "You have my deepest sympathy. It must have been an awful shock to learn the news in such a way. But perhaps it's fortunate your departure was delayed. I'm hoping you might be able to provide us with some key information that could help unravel this mystery."

"I'll do whatever I can, sir. Please ask whatever you wish."

"Let's begin with this: I understand the journey was being made at your father's request?"

"Yes, sir. He sent me a telegram telling me to proceed to Lisbon immediately, and from there to continue by train to Madrid and then on to Barcelona."

"And what was the purpose of this journey?"

"I honestly don't know."

"You don't?"

"No, look—here's the telegram."

Mr Andrews took it and read aloud:

"Proceed immediately Belfast Port embark Esperanza sailing tonight Lisbon. Ultimate destination Barcelona. Further instructions will await you Lisbon. Do not fail. Matter is of utmost importance. Foley."

"There was no prior discussion or correspondence about this?"

Terence shook his head.

"That was the only communication I received. I knew, naturally, that my father had longstanding connections in Spain due to his years living there. But he'd never mentioned sending me there."

"You've spent some time in Spain yourself, haven't you, Mr

Foley?"

"I lived there when I was a child. But I was educated in England and spent most of my holidays there, so in truth, I know less about Spain than you might expect. You see, the War broke out when I was seventeen."

"You served with the English tank division, did you not?"

"Yes, sir."

Mr Andrews nodded thoughtfully and continued with his line of questioning. Terence Foley replied with certainty that he was unaware of any enemies his father may have had in Barcelona or elsewhere in Spain, hadn't noticed any recent changes in his father's behaviour, and had never heard him mention anything resembling a secret. As far as he had believed, the trip to Spain was strictly related to business.

As Mr Andrews paused, Faulkner's calm voice broke the silence. "If you don't mind, magistrate, I'd like to ask a few questions myself."

"Certainly, Mr Faulkner, if you wish," said the magistrate coolly.

Faulkner moved his chair slightly closer to the table.

"Mr Foley, were you on good terms with your father?"

"Of course," the young man replied stiffly.

"You're absolutely sure about that?"

"Yes."

"No disagreements? No quarrels?"

Terence gave a slight shrug. "Everyone has their differences now and then."

"Indeed. But if someone were to claim that you had a heated argument with your father just before your trip to Belfast, that would be entirely untrue?"

I had to admire Faulkner's skill. His earlier claim—*I know everything*—hadn't been empty. Terence Foley was clearly rattled.

"We—we did have an argument," he admitted.

"Ah, an argument. During that exchange, did you say the words, *'When you're dead I can do as I please?'*"

"I might have," he muttered. "I can't say for sure."

"And did your father reply, *'But I'm not dead yet,'* to which you said, *'I wish you were?'*"

The boy didn't answer. His hands fidgeted with the items laid out on the table before him.

"I must insist on an answer, Mr Foley," Faulkner said sharply.

With a flash of anger, Terence swept a heavy paper knife onto the floor.

"What's the use? You may as well hear it. Yes, I did quarrel with my father. Maybe I said all of that—I was so angry I can't even remember! I was furious—so furious I could've killed him in that moment—there, take that as you like!" He leaned back in his chair, face flushed and eyes blazing.

Faulkner gave a slight smile. He pushed his chair back a little and said quietly:

"That's all from me. Mr Andrews, I imagine you'd like to resume your questions?"

"Yes, yes—quite right," Mr Andrews replied. "Now then, may I ask what the quarrel was about?"

"That," Terence said firmly, "I refuse to disclose."

Mr Andrews straightened in his seat.

"Mr Foley, the law is not a matter to be taken lightly," he thundered. "What was the cause of your quarrel?"

Young Foley didn't answer. His youthful features were darkened with resentment. But another voice responded, cool and composed—it was Rupert Mulligan.

"If you like, sir, I can tell you," he said.

"You know the reason?"

"I do indeed. The quarrel was about Madam Ciara Wiffen."

Foley spun around in alarm. The magistrate leaned forward with renewed interest.

"Is that true, sir?"

Terence Foley lowered his head.

"Yes," he said quietly. "I love Madam Wiffen, and I intend to marry her. When I told my father, he immediately flew into a violent temper. Naturally, I couldn't bear to hear him speak ill of the woman I love, and I lost my temper in return."

Mr Andrews looked toward Mrs. Foley.

"Were you aware of this... relationship, madam?"

"I suspected as much," she answered simply.

"Mother!" the boy exclaimed. "You too? Ciara is just as virtuous as she is beautiful. How can you object to her?"

"I don't have any grievance against Madam Wiffen herself. But I would prefer you marry an Englishwoman—or at the very least, not an Irish girl whose mother's background is questionable."

Her dislike for the older Wiffen woman was clear in her tone, and it was easy to see how painful it must have been for her to discover her only son had fallen for the daughter of her long-standing rival.

Mrs. Foley continued, speaking to the magistrate:

"I probably should have brought the matter to my husband's attention, but I hoped it was just a youthful infatuation that would fade more quickly if ignored. I regret my silence now. Still, my husband had seemed so anxious and unlike himself lately that I didn't want to trouble him further."

Mr Andrews gave a small nod.

"So, when you told your father of your intentions regarding Madam Wiffen," he continued, "was he surprised?"

"He was shocked. Then he flatly ordered me to abandon the idea. He said he would never approve of such a marriage. Irritated, I asked what he had against Ciara. He couldn't offer a clear answer, only vague criticisms about the mysterious lives of the Wiffen women. I told him I was marrying Ciara, not her history, but he shut me down and refused to even discuss the matter. The whole relationship had to end. His injustice and heavy-handedness made me furious—especially considering how often he went out of his way to be polite to the Wiffens and insisted they be invited to the clubhouse. I lost control, and we argued heatedly. He reminded me that I was financially dependent on him, and I suppose it was in that moment that I made the comment about doing as I pleased once he was gone—"

Mulligan interjected with a quick question:

"Then you were aware of your father's will?"

"Yes. I knew he had left half his estate to me, with the other half held in trust for my mother and to come to me upon her death," the young man replied.

"Go on," the magistrate instructed.

"After that, we shouted at each other in pure rage until I suddenly realised I was at risk of missing my train to Belfast.

I had to dash for the station, still burning with anger. But once I was away, I started to cool off. I wrote to Ciara and told her what had happened. Her reply calmed me even more. She said we only had to remain steadfast, and the resistance would eventually crumble. Our love had to prove itself. Once my parents understood that this wasn't just a passing fancy, they would come around. Naturally, I didn't tell her the full extent of my father's objections. I quickly saw that violence would get me nowhere."

"Let us move on. Are you familiar with the name Corrigan, Mr Foley?"

"Corrigan?" Terence echoed, puzzled. He leaned forward and slowly retrieved the paper knife he had earlier knocked to the ground. As he lifted his head, his eyes met Faulkner's watchful gaze. "Corrigan? No... I don't believe I know the name."

"Would you mind reading this letter, Mr Foley? Then tell me whether you recognise the sender—whoever addressed it to your father."

Terence took the letter and read through it. As he did, colour rose in his cheeks.

"This was sent to my father?" he asked, his voice thick with emotion.

"Yes. We discovered it in the pocket of his coat."

"Does—" He hesitated, giving the briefest glance toward his mother. The magistrate understood at once.

"She doesn't know. Not yet. Can you identify the writer?"

"I haven't the faintest idea."

Mr Andrews exhaled slowly.

"A very puzzling matter. Well, perhaps we must disregard the letter entirely for now. Now then—ah yes, the weapon. I'm afraid this part may be distressing for you, Mr Foley. As I understand it, the item used was a gift from you to your mother. Most unfortunate—very sad."

Terence leaned forward, his face, which had flushed while reading the letter, now drained of all colour.

"Are you saying—that my father was killed using the tank plate wire paper-cutter I gave my mother? That can't be true! Something so small?"

"Sadly, yes, Mr Foley. A rather ideal weapon, in fact. Sharp, light, and easily handled."

"Where is it now? May I see it? Is it still... with the body?"

"Oh no, it has been removed. You'd like to inspect it? Just to be certain? That seems reasonable—although your mother has already identified it. Still—Mr Blanchflower, would you be so kind?"

"Certainly. I'll bring it at once."

"Wouldn't it be better," Faulkner suggested smoothly, "to take Mr Foley to the shed? Surely he'll want to see his father's body."

The boy gave a slight shudder and shook his head, and the magistrate—seemingly always eager to contradict Faulkner— replied:

"No, not just now. Mr Blanchflower will kindly bring it here."

The inspector left at once. Hall walked over to Terence and clasped his hand firmly. Mulligan had risen and was quietly adjusting a pair of candlesticks, which his meticulous eye had noticed were slightly off-centre. The magistrate, meanwhile, was rereading the mysterious love letter for what must have been the third time, clinging determinedly to his original theory —jealousy, and a stabbing from behind.

Then, without warning, the door flew open and the inspector

rushed back in, breathless.

"Mr Magistrate! Sir!"

"Yes? What is it now?"

"The dagger! It's gone!"

"Gone?" the magistrate repeated, startled.

"Completely vanished. The glass container where it was kept is empty!"

"What?" I exclaimed. "That's impossible. I saw it there myself this morning—" My words faltered and died in my throat.

All eyes in the room turned toward me.

"What did you say?" asked the inspector sharply. "You saw it this morning?"

"Yes," I said slowly. "About an hour and a half ago, to be exact."

"You went to the shed? How did you get the key?"

"I asked the Ulster officer for it."

"And why did you go there?"

I hesitated, but realised honesty was my only option.

"Mr Andrews," I began, "I've made a serious mistake, for which I must ask your pardon."

"Go on," he said.

"Well," I continued, feeling the discomfort rise in me, "I happened to run into a young lady I know. She was very curious and eager to see everything—so, to put it plainly, I took the key to show her the body."

"Ah!" the magistrate cried indignantly. "Captain Lockhart, that is a serious breach of conduct. Entirely irregular. You should not have allowed such a thing."

"I know," I admitted meekly. "There's nothing you could say that I don't deserve."

"You didn't invite this lady here, I assume?"

"Of course not. I encountered her quite by chance. She's an Englishwoman currently staying in Magennis, though I wasn't aware of that until we met unexpectedly."

"Well, well," said the magistrate, his voice softening. "Highly irregular, yes—but the lady is no doubt young and attractive. Ah, youth!" He sighed with sentimental indulgence.

The inspector, less swayed by romanticism and more grounded in the practical, continued the inquiry: "But didn't you lock the door again before leaving?"

"That's the part I blame myself for most," I said slowly. "She was badly shaken by what she saw—almost fainted. I gave her some brandy and water, and then insisted on walking her back to the town. In all the commotion, I forgot to relock the door. I only remembered once I returned to the manor."

"Then for at least twenty minutes..." the inspector murmured. He stopped mid-thought.

"Exactly," I said quietly.

"Twenty minutes," the inspector repeated thoughtfully.

"This is a serious matter," Mr Andrews declared sternly, his tone regaining its edge. "An inexcusable lapse."

Then another voice cut in.

"You find it deplorable?" Faulkner asked.

"Of course," the magistrate snapped.

"I find it admirable," Faulkner replied calmly.

The statement caught me off guard. This unexpected show of

support left me momentarily bewildered.

"Admirable, Mr Faulkner?" the magistrate asked cautiously, eyeing him sideways.

"Indeed."

"And why would that be?"

"Because it proves the murderer—or an accomplice—was near the manor no more than an hour ago. With that information, it should not be difficult to catch them." There was a threatening undertone in his voice. "Whoever it was took a great risk to retrieve that dagger. Perhaps they feared it would reveal fingerprints."

Mulligan turned to Blanchflower.

"You said there weren't any prints?"

Faulkner gave a small shrug. "Perhaps the thief couldn't be sure."

"You're mistaken, Mr Faulkner," Mulligan said. "The killer wore gloves. He would have been confident of that."

"I never claimed it was the killer himself," Faulkner replied. "It may have been an accomplice—someone unaware of that detail."

The magistrate's clerk had begun collecting the papers from the table. Mr Andrews turned to us with a final address.

"Our business here is concluded. Mr Foley, I'd like you to listen as your statement is read back. I've kept these proceedings deliberately informal. Some call my methods unorthodox, but I believe there's value in originality. The case is now in the capable hands of the famous Mr Faulkner. I've no doubt he'll distinguish himself—indeed, I only wonder why he hasn't already caught the culprit! Madam, once more, my sincerest condolences. Gentlemen, good day to you all."

With that, and trailed by his clerk and the inspector, Mr Andrews took his leave.

Mulligan pulled out his large, old-fashioned pocket watch and checked the time.

"Let's head back to the hotel for lunch," he said to me. "And you can tell me all about your scandalous adventure this morning. No one is watching us—we can slip away without farewells."

We slipped out of the room quietly. The magistrate had just driven off in his car. I was descending the steps when Mulligan's voice called me back.

"One moment, my friend."

With remarkable speed, he whipped out his measuring tape and solemnly measured an overcoat hanging in the hallway, from collar to hem. I hadn't noticed it there before and assumed it must belong to either Mr Hall or Terence Foley.

Then, with a small grunt of satisfaction, Mulligan tucked the tape away and followed me out into the open air.

Chapter Twelve

"**W**hy did you measure that overcoat?" I asked, curious, as we walked side by side along the hot, chalk-white road, our pace unhurried.

"Why, to find out its length, of course," Mulligan replied calmly, without missing a beat.

I felt a flare of irritation. Mulligan's incessant habit of making a riddle out of everything never failed to get under my skin. I said nothing and drifted into my own thoughts. Though I hadn't paid them much attention at the time, some of Mrs. Foley's words to her son now echoed in my mind with renewed significance. *"So you did not sail?"* she had said—and then, almost as if to herself, *"After all, it does not matter—now."*

What exactly had she meant by that? Her words were cryptic— weighted. Could it be that she knew more than she had let on? She had claimed ignorance of the secret mission her husband had intended for Terence. But had that been entirely truthful? Was she actually better informed than she pretended? Could she provide answers, if she chose to—and was her silence part of a deliberate, well-calculated plan?

The longer I considered it, the more convinced I became. Mrs. Foley was concealing something. Her shock at her son's unexpected arrival had momentarily caused her to slip. I was certain she knew something—perhaps not the identity of the murderer, but certainly the reason behind the murder. Some powerful motive must be holding her tongue.

"You're thinking deeply, my friend," said Mulligan, breaking into my thoughts. "What is it that's stirring your brain?"

I shared my suspicions with him, half-expecting him to dismiss them. But to my surprise, he nodded gravely.

"You're absolutely right, Lockhart. I've suspected from the start that she was hiding something. In fact, at one point I wondered whether she might have been involved—if not directly, then indirectly, by aiding or encouraging the act."

"You suspected her?" I exclaimed.

"Indeed. After all, she stands to gain a great deal—in fact, under the terms of the new will, she's the sole beneficiary. That alone made her a natural person of interest. Perhaps you noticed I made a point of examining her wrists early on. I needed to see if there was any chance she had tied and gagged herself. But it was immediately clear the bindings were real—the cords had cut into her flesh. That eliminated the possibility that she carried out the crime alone. Still, it remained possible she played a part in it, perhaps with assistance. Besides, her version of events seemed oddly familiar to me—the anonymous masked intruders, the cryptic mention of 'the secret'—I'd come across such claims before in both fact and fiction."

He paused and gave me a meaningful look. "And then there was that other detail. The wristwatch, Lockhart—the wristwatch!"

That wristwatch again! Mulligan was watching me closely.

"Well?" he prompted. "Do you understand?"

"No," I answered shortly. "I don't see it—and I don't pretend to. You always have these blasted mysteries, and there's never any use asking for a straight explanation. You love to keep everything tucked away until the last possible moment."

"Calm yourself, my friend," Mulligan said with a grin. "I'll explain—on one condition. Not a word of this to Faulkner. He treats me like a relic, someone to be brushed aside! We shall see!

Out of fairness, I gave him a hint. If he ignores it, that's his own problem."

I promised him he could trust me.

"Excellent," he said. "Now let us put our little grey cells to work. Tell me, what time do you believe the murder took place?"

"Why, around two o'clock," I replied, surprised at the question. "Mrs. Foley said she heard the clock strike while the men were still in the room."

"Exactly. And based on that alone, you, the magistrate, Blanchflower—everyone—accepted it as fact. But I, Rupert Mulligan, say that Madam Foley lied. The murder happened at least two hours earlier."

"But the medical report—"

"The doctors said death occurred between ten and seven hours before their examination. So the timeline is already flexible. But consider this: for some reason, it was crucial to make the crime appear to have taken place later than it actually did. You've heard of a broken watch or clock being used to suggest the precise hour of a murder, haven't you? In this case, someone tampered with that wristwatch. They moved the hands to two o'clock, then smashed it violently on the floor. But the plan backfired —only the glass shattered; the watch mechanism still worked. That single error told me two things—first, that Madam Foley had lied. Second, that there was a compelling reason to falsify the time."

"But what reason could they possibly have?"

"Ah, and that's the very heart of the puzzle! I don't yet know— but one idea presents itself as plausible."

"And what is it?"

"The last train left Magennis at seventeen minutes past twelve."

I followed his thought slowly.

"Which means... if the murder was believed to occur two hours later, then anyone who boarded that train would have an airtight alibi."

"Exactly, Lockhart! You've grasped it perfectly."

I jumped up.

"Then we must question the station staff! Surely they'd remember if two foreign men boarded that train. We should go there immediately!"

"You really think so, Lockhart?"

"Absolutely. Let's go—right now."

Mulligan held me back gently by the arm.

"By all means, go if you must. But if you do, I wouldn't ask about two foreigners."

I stared at him, confused, and he added with mild exasperation:

"Come now, Lockhart—you don't still believe all that nonsense, do you? The masks, the melodrama, the supposed 'foreigners'— this whole charade?"

His words stunned me so much that I was momentarily lost for a reply. He, however, remained serenely composed and continued on as though he'd merely been discussing the weather:

"You heard me say to Faulkner that all the elements of this crime were familiar to me, did you not?" Mulligan began. "Well, that implies one of two possibilities: either the same mind that orchestrated the earlier crime also planned this one, or the murderer unconsciously reproduced details from a famous case they once read about. I'll be able to say definitively which—once —" He stopped mid-sentence.

My thoughts were occupied elsewhere.

"But what about Mr. Foley's letter?" I said. "It clearly refers to a secret—and to Barcelona!"

"There's no doubt Mr Foley harboured a secret," Mulligan replied. "None whatsoever. But the mention of Barcelona—ah, that's another matter. In my opinion, it's a deliberate distraction, used to mislead both Mr Foley and anyone else looking into the matter. I suspect the same tactic was used on him—to steer his suspicions away from the real source of danger."

He paused and looked at me seriously.

"No, Lockhart. The threat to Mr Foley didn't come from Barcelona. It was much closer—right here in Northern Ireland."

There was such conviction in his tone, such gravity in his expression, that I found myself unable to disagree. Yet one last question lingered.

"And the match and cigarette end found beside the body? What about those?"

A spark of amusement lit Mulligan's eyes.

"Planted! Deliberately placed there for Faulkner or one of his kind to discover! Oh, Faulkner's clever, I grant you that. He knows all the tricks—just like a well-trained hunting dog. He crawls along on his belly for hours, comes back triumphant, and says, 'Look what I've found!' Then he turns to me and asks, 'What do you see here?' And I reply—with complete honesty —'Nothing.' And Faulkner, the great Faulkner, laughs and thinks to himself, 'This old fellow's a fool.' But we shall see... we shall see."

My thoughts drifted back to the core of the case. "Then this whole story about the masked men—?"

"Utter fabrication."

"Then what really happened?"

Mulligan gave a casual shrug.

"There's only one person who could tell us the truth—Madam Foley. But she won't speak. No amount of pressure or pleading would sway her. She's an extraordinary woman, Lockhart. I knew it the moment I laid eyes on her—she's someone of uncommon character. At first, as I said, I suspected she was involved. But later, I changed my mind."

"What made you reconsider?"

"It was the sincerity of her grief when she saw her husband's body. I have no doubt that the pain in her cry was real."

"Yes," I said slowly. "There are certain things you just can't fake."

"My dear friend," said Mulligan, "never assume that. A great actress can portray sorrow so convincingly that it moves even the hardest heart. No, no matter how strong my impression was, I needed more than that before I was satisfied. A truly skilled criminal can also be a brilliant performer. What convinced me beyond question was the fact that Madam Foley actually fainted. I examined her—checked her pulse, lifted her eyelids. It was not feigned. That swoon was genuine. And there was no need for her to fake it, either—she had already had her emotional collapse when told of her husband's death. No one expected a second outburst upon seeing the body. So no, she did not kill her husband."

"But why lie?" I asked. "She lied about the wristwatch. She lied about the masked men. What else?"

"She lied about a third thing," said Mulligan. "Tell me, Lockhart —how do you explain the open door?"

I hesitated. "Well," I admitted, "I suppose they simply forgot to close it."

Mulligan sighed and shook his head.

"That's Faulkner's explanation. I don't buy it. There's a meaning behind that open door—one I haven't quite grasped yet. But one thing I do believe: they didn't exit through it. They left through the window."

"What?" I exclaimed. "Through the window?"

"Precisely."

"But there weren't any footprints in the flowerbed below!"

"No—and there should have been. Now listen. Gerry, the gardener, told us he planted both flowerbeds the afternoon before. One is full of prints—his hobnailed boots. The other has none at all. Doesn't that strike you as odd? Someone passed through that bed and erased their own footprints—using a rake."

"But where would they find a rake?"

"Where they found the spade—and the gardening gloves," Mulligan said briskly. "That's hardly difficult to account for."

"But why are you so sure they exited through the window? Isn't it more likely they came in that way and left through the door?"

"That's certainly a possibility," he conceded. "Still, my instincts say they left by the window."

"I think you're mistaken."

"Perhaps, my dear sir."

I fell silent, turning over the implications of Mulligan's deductions in my mind. Only now did I begin to fully appreciate the significance of his earlier cryptic remarks—the wristwatch, the flowerbed. What had once seemed obscure now revealed an emerging pattern. With a new sense of admiration, I acknowledged how much Mulligan had managed to uncover from a handful of small details.

"And yet," I said slowly, "while we've learned a great deal, we're no closer to discovering who actually committed the murder."

"No," Mulligan said brightly. "In fact, we're much further from it now."

He seemed so pleased by this fact that I stared at him in bewilderment.

He caught my eye and smiled.

Suddenly, a revelation struck me.

"Mulligan! Mrs. Foley—of course! She must be protecting someone."

He didn't react with surprise. His calm reception of the idea told me he had already considered it.

"Yes," he said thoughtfully. "Protecting—or shielding someone. One or the other."

As we stepped into our hotel, he raised a finger to his lips, signalling for silence.

Chapter Thirteen

We ate lunch with hearty appetites. For a while, we dined in silence, until Mulligan commented slyly, "Well? And your morning's indiscretions? You've yet to tell me about them."

I felt myself redden.

"Oh, you mean this morning?" I tried to sound casual and unaffected.

But Mulligan was not so easily deflected. Within moments, he had coaxed the entire tale out of me, his eyes sparkling with mischief as he listened.

"Splendid! A thoroughly romantic episode. What's the name of this delightful young woman?"

I had to admit I didn't know.

"Even more romantic! Your first meeting on the train from Belfast, the second here. 'Journeys end in lovers' meetings'—isn't that the saying?"

"Don't be a fool, Mulligan."

"Yesterday it was Madam Wiffen, today it's Madam Belle! Truly, Lockhart, you have the soul of a Sultan—you should establish a harem!"

"It's easy to mock. Ciara Wiffen is a very beautiful girl, and I do admire her, I'll freely admit that. The other one—well, she's nothing. I doubt I'll ever see her again."

"You don't intend to see her again?"

His tone carried just a hint of interrogation, and I noticed the quick, sharp glance he cast in my direction. In my mind, I saw clearly the words *Cherryhill Hotel*, like writing in flame, and I heard her voice again: *"Come and look me up,"* and my own enthusiastic reply: *"I will."*

I answered Mulligan lightly.

"She invited me to look her up, but I don't plan to."

"And why not?"

"Well, I've no real desire to, that's all."

"She's staying at the Hotel Slieve Donard, isn't she? That's what you told me."

"No—Cherryhill Hotel."

"Ah yes, quite right. I'd forgotten."

A flicker of unease passed through me. Had I actually mentioned any hotel to Mulligan? I was sure I hadn't. But when I looked at him, he seemed fully engrossed in neatly slicing his bread into squares. He must have assumed I'd told him the name.

We had coffee outside, overlooking the sea. Mulligan lit one of his tiny cigarettes and then took out his watch.

"The train to Belfast leaves at 2:25," he said. "I should be getting ready."

"Belfast?" I repeated in surprise.

"That's what I said, my dear fellow."

"You're going to Belfast? Whatever for?"

He replied with complete seriousness: "To search for Mr Foley's killer."

"You believe he's in Belfast?"

"I'm certain he's not. But that's where I must begin my search. You don't understand just yet, but I'll explain everything in due time. Trust me, this trip is essential. I won't be gone long—most likely, I'll return tomorrow. In the meantime, I'd prefer you stay here. Keep an eye on Faulkner, and also get closer to Mr Foley's son."

"That reminds me," I said. "I've been meaning to ask—how did you know about those two?"

"My dear Lockhart, I understand human nature. Put a young man like Foley and a beautiful girl like Ciara together, and what do you expect? Then consider the quarrel—either about money or a woman. From Clare's description of the boy's fury, I guessed it was the latter. I made a deduction—and I was correct."

"You already suspected she had feelings for Foley?"

Mulligan gave a slight smile.

"At the very least, I saw that she had anxious eyes. That's how I always think of Madam Wiffen—*the girl with the anxious eyes.*"

His tone had turned serious, and it unsettled me.

"What do you mean by that, Mulligan?"

"I have a feeling you'll understand before long. But now—I must go."

"I'll come with you to the station," I said, rising from my chair.

"You'll do no such thing. I forbid it."

He was so abrupt, I stared at him.

He nodded firmly. "I mean it. Goodbye."

After he left, I felt at loose ends. I wandered down to the beach and idly watched the dog walkers and mothers with children picking up seashells, but lacked the energy to join them. I half imagined Belle might be there too, dressed in something extravagant and ready to wade into the sea—but she was nowhere to be seen.

Eventually, I drifted along the sands toward the far end of the town. It occurred to me that, out of decency, I ought to at least check in on the girl. It would put the whole matter to rest. Once I'd done so, I could forget all about her. After all, if I didn't make the effort, she might well decide to look *me* up at the clubhouse.

So, I left the beach and walked inland. It didn't take long to locate the Cherryhill Hotel—an unassuming sort of place. It irritated me to no end that I didn't know her name. To save face, I decided I'd simply stroll inside and have a look around. She was probably in the lounge.

I stepped in—but saw no sign of her. I waited for a time, but my patience wore thin. Eventually, I took the concierge aside and quietly pressed a five-pound note into his hand.

"I'm trying to find a young English lady who's staying here— small and dark-haired. I'm afraid I don't know her name."

The man shook his head, a faintly amused look on his face.

"There's no lady matching that description staying here."

"But she told me she was staying here."

"Sir may have misunderstood—or more likely, the lady gave the wrong name. Another gentleman has already been here asking after her."

"What did you say?" I demanded, startled.

"But yes, sir. A gentleman who gave the exact same description as you."

"What did he look like?"

"He was a small gentleman—smartly dressed, very tidy, immaculate even. His goatee was precisely trimmed and pointed, his head had an unusual shape, and his eyes were a striking topaz blue."

Mulligan! So that's why he wouldn't let me go with him to the station. The nerve of the man! I'd appreciate it if he refrained from interfering in my affairs. Did he think I needed a guardian to watch over me?

After thanking the man, I took my leave, still puzzled and more than a little annoyed at my intrusive companion.

But where was the woman? I pushed aside my irritation and tried to reason it out. Perhaps she'd mentioned the wrong hotel by mistake. Yet another possibility surfaced—was it really a mistake? Or had she purposely concealed her identity and misled me with a false address?

The more I dwelled on it, the more convinced I became that the latter was true. For reasons unknown, she clearly had no intention of allowing our encounter to evolve into anything further. And though not long ago I had been of the same mind, I didn't appreciate having the tables turned on me. The whole situation was deeply unsatisfying, and I made my way to the County Golf Course feeling distinctly out of sorts. I didn't head for the clubhouse but instead walked up the path to the small bench beside the shed, where I sat down, brooding.

My thoughts were suddenly interrupted by nearby voices. Within moments, I realized they weren't coming from the garden I was in, but from the adjacent grounds of Manor Carney, and they were drawing nearer. A young woman's voice reached my ears—the unmistakable voice of the beautiful Ciara.

"My love," she said, "is it really true? Are all our troubles over at last?"

"You know it, Ciara," replied Terence Foley. "Nothing can separate us now, my darling. The final barrier between us is gone. No one can take you away from me."

"No one?" she repeated softly. "Oh Terence, Terence—I'm frightened."

Realizing I was unintentionally eavesdropping, I started to rise and slip away. But as I stood, I spotted them through a gap in the hedge. They were facing one another, the man's arm wrapped around the girl, his eyes locked on hers. They made a striking couple—the dark, strongly built youth and the fair-haired beauty. Standing there, they seemed perfectly matched, despite the dark shadow that loomed over their young lives.

Yet worry clouded the girl's expression, and Terence appeared to notice, drawing her closer as he asked:
"What is it, love? What could you possibly fear—now?"

And then I saw the expression in her eyes—the same haunted look Mulligan had described—as she murmured words I could almost make out:
"I'm afraid—for you."

I didn't hear Foley's response, for my attention was drawn to something odd a little farther down the hedge. There, where nothing should have been, was what looked like a brown shrub. It struck me as strange—too early in the season for such foliage. I took a few steps to investigate, but as I approached, the bush suddenly pulled back—and faced me with a raised finger pressed to its lips. It was Faulkner.

Motioning for silence, he led me around the shed to a spot out of earshot.
"What were you doing there?" I demanded.

"Exactly what you were doing—listening."
"But I wasn't there on purpose!"

"Ah," Faulkner said with a smirk. "I was."

As always, I couldn't help but admire him, even while I disliked him. He gave me a once-over, eyes brimming with contempt.

"You didn't help the situation by barging in. I might've picked up something useful if you hadn't interrupted. What have you done with that old relic of yours?"

"Mr Mulligan has gone to Belfast," I said coolly.

Faulkner snapped his fingers with clear disdain. "So he's off to Belfast, is he? Good riddance. The longer he stays there, the better. But what does he expect to find?"

There was a trace of unease in his voice—or so it seemed to me. I straightened.
"I'm not at liberty to say," I replied calmly.

He studied me with a sharp, narrowing gaze.
"He probably had the sense not to tell you," he sneered. "Good day. I've got work to do." And with that, he spun around and walked off without another word.

Things at the County Golf Course appeared to be at a standstill. Faulkner had no desire for my company, and from what I'd witnessed, neither did Terence Foley.

I returned to town, enjoyed a refreshing swim, and headed back to the hotel. I went to bed early, wondering whether the next day would bring anything of note.

I was entirely unprepared for what it did bring. I was having breakfast in the hotel dining room when the waiter, who had just spoken to someone outside, reentered visibly flustered. He hesitated a moment, fiddling nervously with his napkin, before blurting:
"Sir will excuse me, but you're involved in the business at the County Golf Course, are you not?"

"Yes," I answered quickly. "Why?"

"Then sir hasn't heard the latest?"
"What latest?"

"There was another murder there—last night!"

"What?"

Abandoning my breakfast, I grabbed my hat and sprinted out. Another murder—while Mulligan was away! What terrible timing. But who had been the victim?

I rushed through the gate. A small crowd of servants had gathered in the driveway, chattering and gesturing wildly. I caught hold of Rose.

"What's happened?" I demanded.

"Oh, sir! Another death! It's horrible. There's a curse on that clubhouse—I swear it! They ought to bring a priest, sprinkle the place with holy water. I won't spend another night under that roof, no sir. Who knows—it could be me next!"

She crossed herself in fear.
"Yes, but who was killed?" I pressed.

"Me? How would I know? Some man—a stranger. They found him up there, in the shed—not a hundred paces from where the last body was discovered. And that's not the worst of it. He was stabbed—stabbed right through the heart—with the same dagger!"

Chapter Fourteen

Without wasting another moment, I turned and ran up the path toward the shed. The two men standing guard stepped aside to let me pass, and with a sense of urgency and mounting excitement, I entered.

The light inside was dim. The shed itself was little more than a crude wooden structure meant to store old pots and gardening tools. I had entered in a rush, but stopped abruptly on the threshold, drawn to the scene unfolding before me.

Faulkner was crouched on his hands and knees, a small flashlight in hand, carefully inspecting every inch of the floor. At the sound of my arrival, he looked up with a frown, though his expression softened slightly into a kind of condescending amusement.

"There he is," Faulkner said, angling his torch toward the far corner. I walked over.

The body lay on its back, straight and undisturbed. The man appeared to be of medium build, dark-complexioned, and perhaps around fifty. He was neatly dressed in a dark grey suit—well tailored and clearly expensive, though not brand new. His face was twisted in a grimace of agony, and on his left side, just above the heart, a black-handled dagger protruded—gleaming darkly. I recognized it at once. It was the same dagger I had seen resting in the glass jar the previous morning.

"I'm expecting the doctor shortly," Faulkner explained. "Though, honestly, it's a formality. The cause of death is obvious. He was stabbed through the heart—death must have been instant."

"Do you think it happened last night?" I asked.

Faulkner shook his head.
"Unlikely. I'm not giving a medical opinion, mind you, but this man's been dead more than twelve hours. When did you last see that dagger?"

"Yesterday morning—about ten o'clock."

"Then I'd estimate the murder took place not long after that."

"But people were coming and going past this shed all day."

Faulkner gave a low, unpleasant chuckle.
"You're making great progress! And who told you the murder happened inside the shed?"

"Well—" I faltered, caught off guard. "I assumed it."

"What a brilliant detective you'd make! Just look at him. A man stabbed through the heart doesn't collapse so neatly—legs together, arms placed at his sides. And no man lies down calmly to be stabbed without putting up a fight, wouldn't you agree? No—it's nonsense. Now look here, and here—" He moved the torch across the ground, highlighting irregular indentations in the dirt. "He was brought here after he was dead. Dragged—or half carried—by two people. The tracks don't show clearly on the harder ground outside, and here they've been deliberately disturbed. But one of the two was a woman, my young friend."

"A woman?" I echoed.

"Yes."

"But how can you tell if the tracks have been erased?"

"Even smudged, a woman's shoe leaves a distinct print. And then —there's this." He leaned forward, drew something from the dagger's handle, and held it up for my inspection. It was a long strand of black hair—identical to the one Mulligan had retrieved from the armchair in the library.

With a faintly mocking smile, Faulkner wound the hair around the dagger again.
"We'll disturb things as little as possible," he said. "It keeps the examining magistrate happy. Now then—do you see anything else?"

I had to admit I didn't.

"Look at his hands."

I did. The fingernails were broken and stained, the skin rough and hardened. It didn't give me as much insight as I'd hoped. I looked up questioningly.

"Those are not the hands of a gentleman," Faulkner said, reading my expression. "And yet he's dressed like a man of wealth. Strange, isn't it?"

"Very," I agreed.

"None of his garments are marked with initials or tags. That tells us something. This man was pretending to be someone he wasn't. He was in disguise. But why? Was he hiding from something—or someone? Was he trying to disappear? We can't say yet. But this much is clear—he was just as determined to hide his identity as we are to uncover it."

He looked down again at the body.
"As before, no fingerprints on the dagger's handle. The killer wore gloves."

"You think the same person committed both murders?" I asked eagerly.

Faulkner's face became unreadable.
"What I think doesn't matter. We'll see in due time. McGrady!"

The Ulster officer appeared at the door. "Sir?"

"Why isn't Madam Foley here yet? I called for her fifteen minutes ago."

"She's on her way up the path now, sir. Her son is with her."

"Good. But I only want to speak to one of them at a time."

McGrady saluted and left again. Moments later, he returned with Mrs. Foley.

"Here is Madam."

Faulkner stepped forward with a brief nod.
"This way, madam." He guided her over, then suddenly stepped aside. "There is the man. Do you recognize him?"

Even as he spoke, he scrutinized her closely—his sharp eyes drilling into her expression, noting every subtle movement and reaction.

But Mrs. Foley remained utterly composed—too composed, I thought. She glanced at the body with disinterest, showing neither distress nor recognition.

"No," she said calmly. "I've never seen him before. He's a complete stranger to me."

"You're certain?"

"Quite certain."

"You don't recognize him as one of your attackers, perhaps?"
"No." She hesitated, as if the notion had just occurred to her. "No, I don't think so. Of course, they were wearing beards—false ones, the examining magistrate believed—but still, no." She now appeared to reach a firm decision. "I'm certain that neither of the two was this man."

"Very well, madam. That's all for now."

She walked out with her head high, the sunlight glinting on

the silver strands in her hair. Terence Foley followed her in. He, too, failed to recognize the deceased, and his manner seemed entirely genuine.

Faulkner only grunted. Whether he was satisfied or disappointed, I couldn't tell. Then he called out to McGrady.
"You've got the other one there?"
"Yes, sir."
"Bring her in."

"The other" turned out to be Madam Wiffen. She entered with evident outrage, protesting loudly.
"I object to this, sir! It's disgraceful! What has all this to do with me?"

"Madam," Faulkner said sharply, "I'm not investigating one murder, but two. For all I know, you could have committed both."

"How dare you!" she exclaimed. "How dare you insult me with such an outrageous suggestion! It's appalling!"

"Appalling, is it? What about this?" He stooped again, pulled the strand of hair from the dagger's handle, and held it up. "Do you see this, madam?" He stepped toward her. "May I see if it matches?"

With a gasp, she recoiled, her face suddenly drained of colour.
"It's not mine, I swear it. I know nothing about the murder—either of them. Anyone who says otherwise is lying! Oh, Mother Mary, what am I to do?"

"Compose yourself, madam," said Faulkner coolly. "No one has formally accused you. But I suggest you answer my questions clearly and without delay."

"Anything you wish, sir."

"Look at the dead man. Have you ever seen him before?"

She moved closer, some colour returning to her cheeks, and gazed at the body with a mixture of curiosity and concern. Then she shook her head slowly.
"No. I don't know him."

The words sounded entirely natural—too natural to suspect deceit. Faulkner gave a brief nod to dismiss her.

"You're letting her go?" I asked quietly. "Is that wise? That strand of hair—it must be hers."

"I don't need instruction on how to do my job," Faulkner replied dryly. "She's under observation. I see no reason to arrest her just yet."

Then, frowning, he looked down at the corpse.
"Would you say he's of Spanish type?" he asked abruptly.

I studied the face carefully.
"No," I replied after a moment. "He looks Irish to me—definitely."

Faulkner grunted, displeased.
"I thought so too."

He stood still for a moment, then motioned me aside with a curt gesture and resumed his search of the shed floor. Back on his hands and knees, he worked with meticulous attention. Inch by inch, he combed the area, lifting pots, inspecting sacks, examining every corner.

He pounced on a bundle near the door, but it turned out to be just a tattered coat and trousers, which he tossed aside with a snarl. Two pairs of old gloves caught his interest briefly, but in the end, he set them down with a shake of his head. He returned to the pots, lifting and turning them over one at a time with mechanical precision. Finally, he rose to his feet, his expression thoughtful, almost troubled. I don't think he even remembered I was there.

At that moment, we heard movement and chatter outside. The examining magistrate had arrived, accompanied by his clerk, Mr. Blanchflower, and the doctor, who followed just behind.

"This is astonishing, Mr. Faulkner," exclaimed Mr. Andrews. "Another murder! Extraordinary! We clearly haven't uncovered the heart of this case yet. There's something deeply mysterious going on. But who is the victim this time?"

"That's the mystery, sir," Faulkner replied. "No one's been able to identify him."

"Where's the body?" asked the doctor.

Faulkner stepped slightly to the side.
"There—in the corner. Stabbed straight through the heart, as you'll see. With the very same dagger that went missing yesterday morning. My guess is that the murder took place soon after the theft. But you'll have to confirm that. You can examine the weapon as much as you like—there are no fingerprints."

The doctor knelt beside the corpse, while Faulkner turned to address the magistrate.
"A tidy little puzzle, wouldn't you say? But I intend to solve it."

"And no one can identify the man?" the magistrate mused aloud. "Could he have been one of the killers? Perhaps they quarrelled among themselves."

Faulkner shook his head.
"I'd swear he's Irish—without question—"

But the doctor interrupted them. He had settled back on his heels and was wearing a puzzled expression.
"You say he was killed yesterday morning?"

"I estimate the time based on when the dagger disappeared," Faulkner said. "Of course, he might have been killed later that day."

"Later? Nonsense!" the doctor said bluntly. "This man's been dead at least forty-eight hours—probably longer."

We all stared at each other in stunned silence.

Chapter Fifteen

The doctor's statement was so unexpected that we were all momentarily stunned. Here was a man who had been stabbed with a dagger we knew for a fact had only been stolen twenty-four hours earlier, and yet Dr. Fisher had just stated, with complete certainty, that the man had been dead for at least forty-eight hours! The entire situation was bewildering to the extreme.

We were still reeling from the shock of this revelation when a telegram was handed to me. It had been sent up from the hotel to the manor. I tore it open. It was from Mulligan, informing me that he was returning on the train due to arrive at Magennis at 12:28.

A glance at my watch told me I had just enough time to reach the station in comfort and be there to meet him. I felt it was absolutely vital that he be made aware of the latest, astonishing developments in the case as soon as possible.

Clearly, I thought, Mulligan had found what he was looking for in Belfast without difficulty. The speed of his return confirmed that. Just a few short hours had sufficed. I wondered how he would react to the dramatic news I had to share.

The train was running a few minutes behind schedule, so I passed the time by pacing the platform. It occurred to me that I might as well make some inquiries about who had departed Magennis by the last train on the night of the murder.

I approached the head porter, a sharp-looking fellow, and found him quite willing to talk. He was indignant, stating that it was disgraceful that such villains or murderers could roam about without being brought to justice. I hinted that there was some chance the culprits had escaped on the midnight train, but he quickly dismissed the idea. Two foreigners? He'd have noticed them immediately. Only about twenty passengers had boarded that train, and he was sure he would have seen anyone suspicious.

I can't say what prompted the sudden thought—perhaps it was the undercurrent of worry I'd sensed in Ciara Wiffen's voice— but I asked abruptly:

"Young Mr. Foley—he didn't leave on that train, did he?"

"Oh no, sir. To arrive and take off again within half an hour— that would be no fun at all!"

I stared at him, the implications of his words not registering at first. Then the realisation struck me.
"You mean," I said, pulse quickening, "Mr. Terence Foley arrived in Magennis that night?"

"But of course, sir. On the late train from the other direction. The one that comes in at 11:40."

My mind raced. That explained Ciara's anxiety—her apprehension made sense now. Terence Foley had been in Magennis on the night of the murder. But why had he kept that hidden? Why had he allowed us to believe that he had remained in Belfast Port the whole time? I found it hard to reconcile this secrecy with his open, boyish manner. Still, the facts spoke plainly. And clearly, Ciara had known all along— hence her nervousness and her urgent questions to Mulligan about whether anyone had fallen under suspicion.

My reflections were cut short by the sound of the approaching train. Moments later, I was greeting Mulligan as he stepped onto the platform. The little man was radiant. Beaming and animated, he cast aside his usual English restraint and embraced me enthusiastically.

"My dear fellow, I have succeeded—succeeded beyond expectation!"

"Really? I'm glad to hear it. But have you had any word of what's happened here?"

"How could I? What would I have heard? Something's occurred, has it? Has our brave Faulkner made an arrest? Or several, perhaps? Ah, but I shall make him eat his words, that one! But tell me, where are you taking me? Surely we're going to the hotel? I must attend to my goatee—it's quite wilted from the heat. And no doubt my coat is dusty. And my tie—"

I interrupted him, cutting short his complaints.

"My dear Mulligan, never mind all that. We need to go to the clubhouse immediately. There's been another murder."

I've never seen a man look more shocked. His jaw dropped, his cheerfulness vanished. He stared at me in utter disbelief.

"What are you saying? Another murder? Then I was completely mistaken. I've failed. Faulkner may mock me all he likes—he would be justified!"

"You didn't anticipate this, then?"

"Me? Not in the slightest. It blows my entire theory apart—it destroys everything—" He broke off suddenly, striking his chest. "No! It cannot be! I can't be wrong. Taken in logical sequence, the facts admit only one conclusion. I must be correct—I *am* correct!"

"But then—"

"Wait," he said, raising a hand. "I must be right. Therefore, this new murder cannot have occurred—unless... unless—ah, hold on. Say no more, I beg you."

He fell silent for a few moments, then resumed in a calm and confident tone.

"The victim is a middle-aged man. His body was found inside the locked shed, close to the original scene. He had been dead for at least forty-eight hours. He was almost certainly stabbed in a manner similar to Mr. Foley—though perhaps not in the back."

It was my turn to be stunned—and stunned I was. In all my time knowing Mulligan, I had never seen him do anything quite so astonishing. A flicker of doubt crossed my mind.

"Mulligan," I exclaimed, "you're playing a trick on me! You've already heard everything!"

He turned to me with a look of genuine reproach.

"Would I do such a thing? I give you my word—I know nothing of what's occurred here. Didn't you see the shock on my face when you told me?"

"Then how in heaven's name could you possibly know all that?"

"I was right, then? Of course I was! The little grey cells, my friend —the little grey cells! They never lie. Only by this explanation could a second death make any sense. Now, come—tell me everything. If we cut round to the left here, we can take a shortcut across the links that'll bring us out behind the County Golf Course much faster."

As we walked along the path he indicated, I told him everything I knew. Mulligan listened intently, without interruption.

"The dagger was still in the body, you say? That's interesting. You're certain it was the same one?"

"Absolutely. That's what makes the situation so inexplicable."

"Nothing is inexplicable. There might have been two daggers."

I raised an eyebrow.

"That seems incredibly unlikely. Such a coincidence would be astonishing."

"You speak, as usual, without thinking, Lockhart. In many situations, two identical weapons would be improbable, yes—but not here. This particular dagger was a war relic, made specifically to Terence Foley's design. When you think about it logically, it would be far more surprising if he'd only commissioned one. More than likely, he had a second made for his personal use."

"But no one has mentioned anything about another dagger," I protested.

A trace of lecture crept into Mulligan's voice.

"My dear fellow, one does not work a case by relying only on what people 'mention.' There are many important details that go unspoken—and just as often, there's good reason why they're not spoken of. You can choose which motive applies in this case."

I said nothing, reluctant but impressed. A few more minutes brought us to the notorious shed. We found everyone still there, and after a few formal greetings were exchanged, Mulligan got to work.

Having watched Faulkner in action earlier, I was eager to see how Mulligan would proceed. Surprisingly, he barely glanced at the surroundings. The only item he bothered to inspect was the bundle of worn clothing near the door. Faulkner smirked slightly, but as if noticing the expression, Mulligan let the garments fall again with a dismissive flick.

"Gardener's old clothes?" he asked.

"Exactly," replied Faulkner.

Mulligan knelt beside the body. His movements were quick, yet precise. He examined the material of the clothing and checked that there were no identifying marks. He paid particular attention to the boots, then to the broken, dirty fingernails. While scrutinizing the latter, he threw a sharp question over his shoulder.

"You saw the hands?"

"Yes," replied Faulkner, his face unreadable.

Suddenly Mulligan froze.

"Dr. Fisher!"

"Yes?" The doctor stepped forward.

"There's foam on the lips. Did you observe that?"

"I must confess, I didn't notice it."

"But you do now?"

"Oh yes—certainly."

Mulligan turned again to Faulkner. "You noticed it too, I presume?"

Faulkner didn't respond. Mulligan carried on. The dagger had been removed and now rested in a glass jar beside the corpse. He examined the weapon, then turned his attention to the wound. When he looked up, his eyes were bright and gleaming with that unmistakable green fire.

"It's a peculiar wound. There's been no bleeding. Not a trace on the clothes. The blade itself is only slightly stained. Doctor, what do you make of that?"

"It's highly unusual," the doctor admitted.

"It's not unusual at all. In fact, it's perfectly straightforward. The man was stabbed after death."

The wave of startled voices that rose in response was halted by a single authoritative gesture from Mulligan. Then he turned to Faulkner and added:

"Mr. Faulkner, you agree with me, don't you?"

Whether Faulkner genuinely agreed or not, he showed no reaction. His reply came cool and steady:
"Certainly. I agree."

Another ripple of murmuring ran through the shed.

"What an extraordinary idea!" exclaimed Mr. Andrews. "To stab a dead man! It's savage—unheard of! Perhaps a crime of deep-seated hatred?"

"No," said Mulligan. "I imagine it was done quite dispassionately —intended to send a message."

"What kind of message?"

"The kind it nearly succeeded in sending," Mulligan replied cryptically.

Mr. Blanchflower, who had been thinking, spoke up.
"But if he wasn't killed by the dagger—how did he die?"

"He wasn't killed at all," said Mulligan calmly. "He died of natural causes. I believe he suffered a fatal epileptic seizure."

This claim provoked another surge of discussion. Dr. Fisher returned to the body and examined it carefully. Finally, he stood up again.

"Mr. Mulligan, I think you're right. I was misled at first. The presence of the stab wound threw me off, but now that I look more closely, the signs are there."

Mulligan had become the man of the hour. The examining magistrate showered him with praise. Mulligan accepted it with poise, then excused himself, reminding everyone that neither he nor I had eaten yet and that the journey had left him in need of refreshment.

As we turned to leave the shed, Faulkner approached with that smooth, slightly taunting tone of his.

"One last thing, Mr. Mulligan. We found this wound around the dagger's handle—a strand of a woman's hair."

"Ah!" said Mulligan. "A woman's hair, you say? I wonder whose."

"I wonder as well," Faulkner replied, with a slight bow, and walked off.

"He's persistent, our friend Faulkner," Mulligan murmured as we headed for the hotel. "Now what misdirection is he hoping to feed me this time? A woman's hair—hmm!"

We ate a hearty lunch, though I found Mulligan unusually quiet and distracted. Afterwards, we returned to our sitting room upstairs, and I pressed him to reveal what he had uncovered on his mysterious trip to Belfast.

"Gladly, my friend. I went to Belfast in search of this." He pulled a small, worn newspaper clipping from his pocket and handed it to me. It featured an old photograph of a woman. I gave an involuntary cry.

"You recognise her, don't you?"

I nodded. Though the photo was clearly very old, and the hairstyle different, the resemblance was unmistakable.

"Madam Wiffen!" I said.

Mulligan smiled and shook his head.

"Not quite. She wasn't known by that name back then. This is a photograph of the infamous Madam Kinahan."

Madam Kinahan! Instantly, it all came flooding back—the sensational murder trial that had once gripped the entire world.

The Kinahan Case.

Chapter Sixteen

Roughly twenty years before the events of this story begin, Mr. Edward Kinahan arrived in Belfast with his attractive young wife and their infant daughter. A native of Dublin, Kinahan was a junior partner in a small wine merchant business—a portly, middle-aged man with a fondness for good food and drink, devoted to his wife, and altogether an ordinary individual. The firm did respectable business, but its size meant that Mr. Kinahan's share was modest. He and his family rented a small flat and began their life in Belfast in a quiet, unassuming fashion.

But while Mr. Kinahan himself was quite unremarkable, his wife was another matter entirely. Young, strikingly beautiful, and blessed with a certain captivating charm, Madam Kinahan quickly attracted attention. Whispers began to circulate—tales of a mysterious past. Some said she was the illegitimate child of a Tuscan Grand Duke. Others claimed she was the legal, though morganatic, daughter of a Hungarian Archduke. Whatever the truth, all versions agreed on one point: Lisa Kinahan was surrounded by intrigue and romantic mystery.

Among the Kinahans' acquaintances was a young solicitor named Caolan Reid. It soon became clear that Lisa Kinahan had won his heart completely. She encouraged him, discreetly but unmistakably, all the while maintaining her expressions of deep loyalty to her much older husband. Nevertheless, gossip spread rapidly, and many claimed that Reid was not only her admirer—but her lover. Nor, they whispered, was he the only one.

Three months after their arrival in Belfast, another key figure entered the picture—Mr. Charlie T. Richards, a wealthy American with substantial means. Introduced to the enigmatic and alluring Madam Kinahan, he quickly fell under her spell. His admiration was unmistakable, though his conduct remained entirely proper.

Around this time, Lisa Kinahan became more candid in her private conversations. To various friends, she expressed concern for her husband's well-being, hinting that he had been drawn into politically sensitive affairs. She referred cryptically to important documents that had been entrusted to him—papers said to contain secrets of immense significance for European security. They had been placed in his care to divert attention from their true owners, but Lisa was nervous. She claimed to have spotted known members of a Revolutionary Circle right there in Belfast.

Then, on the 28th of November, disaster struck. The Kinahans' housekeeper—who came daily to clean and cook—arrived to find the apartment door wide open. Hearing faint groans from the bedroom, she entered—and was met with a horrifying sight. Lisa Kinahan lay on the floor, bound hand and foot, her gag partially dislodged, allowing her to make feeble sounds. On the bed lay Edward Kinahan, in a pool of blood, a knife driven through his heart.

Madam Kinahan gave a straightforward account. She said she'd been roused from sleep to find two masked men standing over her. Before she could cry out, they gagged and bound her. They then demanded that her husband hand over the "secret." The steadfast wine merchant refused. Enraged, one of the men stabbed him fatally. Using his keys, the intruders opened the household safe, removed a collection of documents, and fled. Lisa insisted both men were bearded and masked—and she was certain they were Italians.

The murder caused a tremendous public sensation. Yet despite thorough investigations, the mysterious intruders were never found. Eventually, the buzz began to quiet—until a shocking twist reignited the nation's interest: Madam Kinahan was arrested and charged with her husband's murder.

When the trial began, it captured widespread attention. The youth and beauty of the accused, combined with her exotic reputation, made the case headline material.

In court, it was proven beyond dispute that Lisa Kinahan's parents were humble and respectable fruit sellers living on the outskirts of Dublin. The grand-ducal parentage, the royal liaisons, the political intrigue—all of it had originated from Lisa herself. Piece by piece, her fabricated identity was dismantled. The supposed motive? Mr. Charlie T. Richards. Though he did his best to defend her, he was forced, under rigorous cross-examination, to admit that he loved her. He confessed that if she had been free, he would have asked her to marry him. The fact that he had not acted improperly strengthened the case against Lisa. Unable to win him as a mistress due to his principled nature, she had allegedly plotted the murder of her unimpressive husband to become Mrs. Richards.

Throughout the proceedings, Madam Kinahan remained composed and defiant. Her story never wavered. She persisted in claiming she was of noble descent and had been swapped at birth with the fruit seller's child. The tale was absurd and completely unsubstantiated—but remarkably, many people chose to believe it wholeheartedly.

But the prosecution would not be swayed. They dismissed the tale of the masked "Italians" as a fabrication and argued that the murder had been carried out by Madam Kinahan and her lover, Caolan Reid. A warrant for Reid's arrest was issued, but he had already vanished without a trace.

Evidence presented in court revealed that the bindings used to restrain Madam Kinahan were so loosely tied that she could easily have escaped from them.

Then, near the end of the trial, an anonymous letter was delivered to the Public Prosecutor. Posted in Belfast, it was signed by none other than Caolan Reid. Though he did not disclose his location, the letter contained a complete confession. Reid admitted that it was he who had delivered the fatal stab—at the instigation of Madam Kinahan. The murder, he claimed, had been carefully planned between them.

Believing that Lisa Kinahan was suffering under her husband's cruel treatment, and driven by the overwhelming belief that she returned his love, Reid had plotted the crime and carried it out, convinced he was rescuing the woman he adored. But it was only after the deed was done that he learned of Mr. Charlie T. Richards —and with that revelation came the bitter truth: the woman he had killed for had deceived him. It wasn't for his sake that she wanted her husband gone, but so she could wed the wealthy American. Used as a pawn in her game, Reid now turned against her in a jealous fury, publicly accusing her and claiming he had acted entirely under her influence.

At that point, Madam Kinahan demonstrated the remarkable control and presence of mind for which she was becoming infamous. Without hesitation, she abandoned her previous defence and admitted that the story of the masked Italians was a complete fabrication. The real killer, she now said, was indeed Caolan Reid. Consumed by passion, he had murdered her husband and threatened to take revenge on her if she spoke a word. Terrified by his threats—and fearing she might be accused as an accomplice if she revealed the truth—she had kept silent. But she swore that, following the crime, she had refused all contact with Reid. It was this rejection, she claimed, that had prompted his confession letter, written in vengeance. She solemnly declared that she had no part in planning the murder, and that she had awoken that dreadful night to find Reid standing over her, knife in hand, her husband already dead.

It was a narrow escape. Madam Kinahan's version of events strained belief. But when she stood to address the jury, she delivered a speech that was nothing short of brilliant. Tears streaming down her cheeks, she spoke movingly of her daughter, of her honour as a woman, of her deep need to preserve her name for her child's sake. She admitted that Reid had once been her lover, and that she might be seen as morally culpable—but before God, she claimed, she was innocent of the crime itself. She had been wrong to stay silent, yes—but how could she, a woman who had once loved him, bring herself to send a man to the guillotine? Her voice broke as she declared that no woman could do such a thing. She had made mistakes—serious ones—but she was not guilty of murder.

Whatever the full truth may have been, her words, her charisma, and her emotional appeal carried the jury. Amid scenes of wild excitement, Madam Kinahan was acquitted.

Despite the best efforts of law enforcement, Caolan Reid was never found. As for Madam Kinahan, she disappeared from Belfast, taking her child with her, and vanished to begin life anew.

Chapter Seventeen

I've set out the Kinahan case in full. Naturally, all the details didn't return to me as clearly at the time as I've recounted them here, but I remembered the case reasonably well. It had drawn enormous attention back when it occurred and had been extensively covered in the English press, so recalling the key elements didn't require a great feat of memory.

In my excitement, it momentarily felt as though everything had suddenly fallen into place. I admit I'm impulsive—Mulligan often criticises me for leaping to conclusions—but in this case, I believe I had some justification. The way this new information aligned with Mulligan's theory struck me immediately.

"Mulligan," I said, "congratulations. I understand it all now."

Mulligan lit one of his slim cigarettes with his usual care, then looked up at me.
"And since you now understand everything, my good sir, what is it exactly that you understand?"

"Why, that Madam Wiffen—Madam Kinahan—was the one who killed Mr. Foley. The parallels between the two cases prove it without question."

"So you believe that Madam Kinahan was wrongly acquitted? That she truly was involved in her husband's murder?"

I looked at him, surprised.
"Of course! Don't you?"

Mulligan walked to the far end of the room, adjusted a chair that was slightly out of place, and replied thoughtfully:

"Yes, that happens to be my opinion. But it's far from an 'of course,' my friend. Legally speaking, Madam Kinahan is innocent."

"Innocent of that particular crime, perhaps. But not this one."

Mulligan returned to his seat and regarded me closely, his contemplative manner more intense than ever.
"So, to be clear—it's your firm belief that Madam Wiffen murdered Mr. Foley?"

"Yes," I replied confidently.

"And your reason?"

He shot the question at me so abruptly that I stumbled.

"My reason? Well—because—" I faltered, trailing off.

Mulligan gave a small nod.

"You see? You run into a wall straightaway. Why would Madam Wiffen—let's stick with that name for clarity—kill Mr. Foley? There's not a trace of motive. She gains nothing from his death. Whether considered as a lover or as a blackmailer, she only loses by it. You can't have a murder without a motive. The previous case was different—there we had a wealthy suitor ready to take the husband's place."

"But money isn't the only motive for murder," I protested.

"Quite true," Mulligan agreed placidly. "There are two other broad categories. One is the crime of passion. The other is murder prompted by an idea—what I call abstract motive. That generally involves a mental imbalance. Religious mania, delusional obsession, homicidal madness—they fall under that umbrella. We can rule that out in this case."

"But what about passion? Couldn't that apply? If Madam Wiffen *was* Mr. Foley's mistress, and if she suspected his affections were waning—or if jealousy got the better of her—might she not have lashed out in a moment of rage?"

Mulligan shook his head.

"If—and I stress *if*—Madam Wiffen was involved with Foley, the relationship was far too recent for her to feel rejected. Besides, you're misreading her nature. She's a woman capable of displaying deep emotion—but only as a performance. She's a superb actress. But when you strip away the performance and examine her actions, a different picture emerges. Her history is one of calculation and cold resolve. She didn't conspire to murder her husband out of love for a young man. It was the wealthy American she had her sights on—someone she probably didn't care for at all. But he had money, and that was enough. If she ever commits a crime, it will always be for gain. And in this case, there was none. Add to that—the matter of the grave. That wasn't dug by a woman."

"She might have had help," I argued, unwilling to abandon the theory.

"Let me move on to another objection," Mulligan said. "You spoke of similarities between the two cases. What are they, exactly?"

I stared at him, stunned.

"But Mulligan—it was *you* who first pointed them out! The tale of the masked men, the 'secret,' the missing papers!"

Mulligan gave a faint smile.

"No need to be so indignant. I'm not denying anything. The parallels in the stories do connect the two events unmistakably. But consider something peculiar—it isn't Madam Wiffen who tells that story. If it were, things would be simpler. Instead, it's Madam Foley who repeats it. Are you suggesting the two are in league?"

"I can't believe that," I said slowly. "If they are, then Mrs. Foley is the greatest actress the world has ever seen."

"Ta-ta-ta," Mulligan said with irritation. "You're doing it again—responding with feeling, not logic. If it were necessary for her to be a world-class actress to carry it off, then let's assume she is one. But *is* it necessary? I don't think so. I don't believe for a moment that Mrs. Foley and Madam Wiffen are conspiring together—and I've given you several reasons already. The rest should be obvious. Eliminate that possibility, and we draw closer to the truth—a truth that, as always, is both strange and fascinating."

"Mulligan," I said excitedly, "how much more do you know?"

"My dear sir, you must make your own deductions. You have access to the facts. Use your grey cells. Apply your reason—not like Faulkner—but like Rupert Mulligan!"

"But are you certain?"

"My friend, in many ways I've been a fool. But now—yes, now I see clearly."

"So you know everything?"

"I've discovered what Mr. Foley brought me here to uncover."

"And you know who the murderer is?"

"I know *one* murderer."

"One?" I echoed. "What do you mean?"

"We're talking slightly at cross-purposes," Mulligan replied. "There aren't merely one, but *two* crimes in this affair. The first I have solved. The second—well, I must admit, I'm not yet certain."

"But Mulligan—I thought you said the man in the shed died a natural death?"

"Ta-ta-ta!" Mulligan uttered his favourite expression of

exasperation. "You still don't understand. A single crime might exist without a murderer—but two crimes require two bodies."

The remark struck me as so oddly phrased that I looked at him with concern. But Mulligan appeared perfectly composed. Abruptly, he walked over to the window.

"Here he comes now," he said casually.

"Who?" I asked.

"Mr. Terence Foley. I sent a note up to the clubhouse asking him to come here."

That shifted the direction of my thoughts. I asked Mulligan whether he was aware that Terence Foley had been in Magennis on the night of the murder. I had hoped to catch my perceptive friend off guard for once—but, as always, he was a step ahead. He had already made inquiries at the railway station.

"And doubtless, my dear Lockhart, we were not the only ones struck by that idea. The ever-thorough Faulkner has almost certainly done the same."

"You don't think—" I began, then stopped short. "No, it's too awful to contemplate."

Mulligan gave me a questioning look, but I said no more. A chilling realisation had struck me. Among the seven women connected with the case—Mrs. Foley, Madam Wiffen and her daughter, the mysterious visitor, and the three female servants —there was, apart from old Gerry, who could hardly count, only one man. Terence Foley. And someone had dug a grave.

I didn't have time to pursue the dreadful thought further, for Terence Foley was shown into the room.

Mulligan greeted him with his usual briskness.

"Please sit down, Mr. Foley. I do regret troubling you, but I'm afraid the atmosphere at the manor house is not exactly to my liking. Mr. Faulkner and I disagree on a number of points, and his cordiality toward me has been, shall we say, less than abundant. You will understand, I'm sure, that I have no intention of sharing any discoveries I make with him."

"Completely understandable, Mr. Mulligan," the young man replied. "Faulkner is an unpleasant brute. I'd be more than happy to see someone get the better of him."

"Then perhaps you'll do me a small favour?"

"Certainly."

"I'd like you to take the train to the next station along the line —Abbalac. Inquire at the cloakroom whether two foreigners left a valise there on the night of the murder. It's a quiet station; they're almost certain to remember if anything of the sort occurred. Will you do that for me?"

"Of course," said Foley, clearly puzzled but willing.

"My friend and I, you see, have other business to attend to," Mulligan added. "There's a train in fifteen minutes, and I'd prefer it if you didn't return to the manor afterwards. I don't want Faulkner to catch wind of your errand."

"Understood. I'll go straight to the station," the boy replied, rising to leave.

Mulligan's voice stopped him at the door.

"One last thing, Mr. Foley. Something has puzzled me. Why did you neglect to mention to Mr. Andrews this morning that you were in Magennis the night your father was murdered?"

Foley's face flushed deep red. He composed himself with effort.

"You're mistaken. I was in Belfast Port, as I told the magistrate this morning."

Mulligan narrowed his eyes, catlike, until only a glint of green showed.

"Then I've made an extraordinary error—one shared, strangely enough, by the station staff, who say you arrived on the 11:40 train."

Foley hesitated briefly, then straightened with a defiant look.

"And if I did? Are you suggesting I had some part in my father's death?"

"I'd like to know what brought you here that night."

"That's simple enough. I came to see my fiancée, Madam Wiffen. I was about to leave on a long voyage, uncertain of when I'd return. I wanted to see her—to reaffirm my devotion."

"And did you see her?" Mulligan asked, his eyes still locked on the young man's face.

There was a brief pause.

"Yes," he said finally.

"And after that?"

"I discovered I'd missed the last train. I walked to Clough, woke up a garage owner, and hired a car back to Belfast Port."

"Clough? That's fifteen kilometres away. Quite the hike."

"I—I felt like walking."

Mulligan nodded as if satisfied. Terence picked up his hat and cane and left. The moment the door closed behind him, Mulligan was on his feet.

"Quick, Lockhart—we're going after him."

We followed him at a distance through the streets of Magennis, careful not to be seen. But when Mulligan observed that Foley had taken the turn toward the station, he slowed his pace and smiled.

"All is well. He's taken the bait. He's heading for Abbalac, and he'll ask about the imaginary valise left by the imaginary foreigners. Yes, my dear Lockhart, that was a little fabrication of my own."

"You just wanted him out of the way!" I exclaimed.

"Your insight is dazzling, Lockhart," Mulligan said dryly. "Now, if you'll be so kind, we're heading to the County Golf Course."

Chapter Eighteen

Upon arrival at the manor, Mulligan took the lead, guiding us toward the shed where the second body had been found. He didn't enter, however, choosing instead to stop beside the bench I previously mentioned, situated a few yards away. After a brief pause to examine it, he paced deliberately from the bench to the hedge that served as the border between the County Golf Course and Manor Carney. Then he retraced his steps, nodding thoughtfully. Once more, he returned to the hedge and carefully parted the foliage with his hands.

"With a bit of luck," he said over his shoulder to me, "Madam Ciara may be in the garden. I wish to speak with her and would rather avoid paying a formal visit to Manor Carney. Ah, we're in luck—there she is. Pst, Madam! Pst! Just a moment, if you please."

I joined him just as Ciara Wiffen, looking slightly alarmed, hurried over to the hedge in response to his call.

"A brief word with you, madam, if you don't mind?"

"Of course, Mr Mulligan."

Despite her willingness, there was a troubled, anxious look in her eyes.

"Do you recall running after me on the road the day I visited your home with the examining magistrate? You asked whether anyone had fallen under suspicion."

"And you told me it was two Cataloniaans," she answered, her voice a bit short of breath as her left hand moved to her chest.

"Would you ask me that same question again, madam?"

"What are you suggesting?"

"This: if you were to repeat your question today, my answer would be different. Someone is now under suspicion—and it is not a Cataloniaan."

"Who?" The word left her lips barely above a whisper.

"Mr Terence Foley."

"What?" she cried. "Terence? That's not possible. Who would dare accuse him?"

"Faulkner."

"Faulkner!" Her face turned pale. "That man terrifies me. He's heartless. He'll—he'll—" She trailed off. But something was changing in her expression—resolve began to replace fear. I saw in that moment she was not one to back down. Mulligan, too, was watching her carefully.

"You do know he was present the night of the murder?" Mulligan asked.

"Yes," she replied dully. "He told me."

"It was a mistake trying to hide that fact," Mulligan remarked gently.

"Yes, yes," she said quickly. "But there's no use wasting time on what's done. We need something that can clear his name. I know he's innocent, but with someone like Faulkner—he'll want to preserve his reputation. He needs to arrest someone, and that person will be Terence."

"The evidence points in his direction," Mulligan said. "You understand that?"

She looked directly at him.

"I'm not a child. I can face facts. He's innocent, and we must find a way to prove it."

Her voice carried a fierce determination, then she fell silent, her brow furrowed in thought.

"Madam," Mulligan said, watching her closely, "is there something you haven't yet told us?"

She nodded, looking confused.

"Yes, there is something, though I'm not sure you'll believe me— it sounds so far-fetched."

"Please tell us anyway, madam."

"Well... Mr Faulkner called me later, almost as an afterthought, to see if I could identify the man inside the shed." She gestured toward it with her head. "I couldn't. At least not at the time. But the memory's been coming back to me..."

"Yes?"

"It sounds strange, but I'm almost certain now. On the morning Mr Foley was killed, I was walking in the garden when I overheard raised voices. Two men arguing. I pulled the bushes aside to see who it was. One was Mr Foley. The other was a tramp—a filthy man in rags. He kept switching between begging and threatening. I gathered he was demanding money. Just then, madam called me from the house, and I had to leave. That's all. But—I'm nearly sure the tramp and the dead man in the shed are one and the same."

Mulligan let out a sharp exclamation.

"But why didn't you mention that at the time, madam?"
"Because at first, the face just seemed vaguely familiar. The man looked completely different—his clothing suggested he belonged to a much higher class."

A voice called out from the house.

"Madam," Ciara whispered urgently, "I have to go." She slipped away quickly through the trees.

"Come," said Mulligan, taking my arm and turning us toward the manor.

"What do you honestly think?" I asked, curious. "Was her story true, or was it made up to shift suspicion away from her lover?"

"It's a strange story," Mulligan admitted, "but I'm inclined to believe every word. In fact, without realizing it, Madam Ciara confirmed something else—and exposed Terence Foley's dishonesty. Did you notice how he hesitated when I asked whether he'd seen her on the night of the murder? He paused— then said 'Yes.' That struck me as suspicious. I needed to speak to Madam Ciara before he could warn her.

Three simple words told me what I needed: when I asked her if she knew Terence had been here that night, she replied, 'He told me.' Now think, Lockhart—what was Terence Foley doing at the manor that night, and if he didn't see Ciara, who did he see?"

"You can't seriously be suggesting," I exclaimed in horror, "that a boy like that would murder his own father!"

"My dear fellow," Mulligan said flatly, "your sentimentality knows no bounds. I've seen mothers kill their own children just to collect insurance money. After that, nothing surprises me."

"And the motive?"

"Money, naturally. Don't forget—Terence Foley expected to inherit half his father's wealth when the old man died."

"But what about the tramp? Where does he fit in?"

Mulligan shrugged.

"Faulkner's view is likely that he was an accomplice—some

street thug who helped Foley with the murder and was later eliminated to cover the tracks."

"And the hair around the dagger? The long hair? A woman's hair?"

"Ah!" Mulligan said with a broad grin. "That's the best part of Faulkner's little theory. According to him, it's not a woman's hair at all. Young men these days brush their hair straight back and use pomade or tonic to keep it flat. That often results in a few strands being quite long."

"You believe that explanation?" I asked.

"No," Mulligan replied, a curious smile playing at his lips. "Because I know it is a woman's hair—and more than that, I know whose."

"Madam Wiffen," I said confidently.

"Possibly," Mulligan said, eyeing me with amusement. I resisted the urge to be annoyed.

"So what now?" I asked as we stepped into the main hall of the County Golf Course.

"I want to examine Terence Foley's personal belongings. That's why I had to make sure he was kept away for a while."

Methodically, Mulligan opened each drawer, inspecting its contents with care and returning everything precisely as it had been. It was a slow, tedious process, and the items—collars, pyjamas, socks—offered little insight.

A gentle purring from outside caught my ear, and I moved to the window. Suddenly, I was alert.

"Mulligan!" I shouted. "A car just pulled up. Faulkner's inside—with Terence Foley and two constables!"

"Damnation," Mulligan muttered. "That beast Faulkner—he

couldn't wait! I won't have time to put the contents of this last drawer back properly. Quick, let's finish."

He hastily dumped the contents—mostly ties and handkerchiefs —onto the floor. Then, with a triumphant cry, he snatched up a small square piece of cardboard—a photograph, clearly. Shoving it into his pocket, he swept the other items roughly back into the drawer. Grabbing my arm, he dragged me out of the room and down the stairs.

Faulkner stood in the entrance hall, his eyes fixed on his prisoner.

"Good afternoon, Mr Faulkner," said Mulligan coolly. "What's this?"

Faulkner nodded toward Terence.

"He was trying to escape, but I was too quick for him. He's under arrest—for the murder of his father, Mr Michael Foley."

Mulligan spun around to face the boy, who stood slumped against the doorway, his complexion ghostly pale.

"What do you have to say for yourself, young man?"

Terence Foley looked back with a blank stare.

"Nothing," he said.

Chapter Nineteen

I was stunned. Right up until the last moment, I hadn't truly believed Terence Foley was guilty. I had anticipated a forceful denial, a bold declaration of innocence, when Mulligan confronted him. But now, watching him lean pale and limp against the wall, and hearing that damning admission pass his lips, my doubts vanished.

Mulligan, however, had turned his attention to Faulkner.
"On what grounds have you arrested him?" he asked.
"You expect me to tell you?" Faulkner retorted.
"As a professional courtesy, yes."

Faulkner hesitated, torn between the temptation to dismiss the request with contempt and the desire to revel in his triumph over Mulligan.

"I suppose you think I've made a mistake?" he sneered.
"It wouldn't surprise me," Mulligan said coolly, a touch of acid in his tone.

Faulkner's face darkened with irritation.
"Well then, come with me. You can judge for yourself."

He threw open the door to the salon, and we followed him inside, leaving Terence in the custody of the two constables.

"Now, Mr Mulligan," Faulkner said, placing his hat on the table and speaking with biting sarcasm, "allow me to give you a little demonstration in modern detective work. A masterclass, if you will."
"Hah!" Mulligan said, settling into a chair. "Then permit me to

demonstrate how gracefully the old school can listen." He leaned back, closing his eyes briefly before opening them again to add, "Don't worry—I won't drift off. You'll have my full attention."

"Right then," Faulkner began. "It was clear from the start that all that Catalonian nonsense was a distraction. There were two men involved, but they weren't mysterious foreigners. That was all a smokescreen."

"A solid start, my dear Faulkner," murmured Mulligan. "Especially after their clever trick with the cigarette end and the match."

Faulkner shot him a glare but pressed on.

"A man had to be involved to dig that grave. No one directly benefited from the murder, but there was someone who believed he would—Terence Foley. I learned of his falling out with his father, and the threats he made. So the motive was there.

"As for opportunity—he was in Magennis that night. He hid that fact, which confirmed my suspicions. Then we found the second body—killed with the same dagger. We can determine the exact time the dagger was stolen, thanks to Captain Lockhart here. Terence arrived from Belfast Port, and he was the only one unaccounted for who could have taken it. Every other club member's movements have been verified."

Mulligan interrupted.

"You're wrong. One other person could've taken it."

"You're referring to Mr Hall? He came to the front entrance in a car that brought him directly from Belfast. I checked thoroughly. Terence Foley, on the other hand, came by train. There was an hour between his arrival and when he appeared at the clubhouse. Clearly, he saw Captain Lockhart and his companion leave the shed, slipped in, stole the dagger, and stabbed his accomplice—"

"Who was already dead," Mulligan cut in.

Faulkner shrugged.

"Possibly. He may have assumed the man was sleeping. No doubt they planned to meet. Either way, he knew this supposed second murder would further muddle the case. And it did."

"But not enough to mislead Mr Faulkner," Mulligan murmured.

"You mock me! But here's the clincher—Madam Foley's statement was a complete fabrication. She loved her husband, supposedly, yet she lied to protect his killer. Why would a woman lie? Sometimes for herself, often for a man she loves, but always for her child. That's the key. The ultimate, irrefutable proof. You can't refute it."

Faulkner ended his case, flushed and clearly pleased with himself. Mulligan watched him in silence.

"That's your case?" he asked. "I've only one question."

"And that is?"

"Terence Foley would've known the golf course plans. He knew the body would be discovered almost immediately once they began digging the bunker."

Faulkner let out a sharp laugh.

"That's absurd! He *wanted* the body found. Without a body, he couldn't prove death and thus couldn't claim his inheritance."

Mulligan's eyes glinted with a flash of something fierce as he stood.

"Then why bury it?" he asked softly. "Think about it, Faulkner. If it was in Terence's interest for the body to be discovered quickly, why go to the trouble of burying it at all?"

Faulkner didn't reply. The question caught him off guard. He shrugged, as though brushing it aside.

Mulligan moved to the door, and I followed.

"There's one more detail you've overlooked," Mulligan said over his shoulder.

"And what's that?"

"The length of lead piping," Mulligan answered, and exited.

Terence Foley remained in the hallway, his face a blank, pale mask. But as we came out of the salon, he looked up suddenly. At that same moment, footsteps echoed from the staircase—Mrs Foley was descending.

She froze at the sight of her son flanked by law officers. "Terence?" she whispered. "Terence, what is happening?"

He looked at her, his face rigid.
"They've arrested me, Mother."
"What?"

She let out a piercing scream and collapsed before anyone could reach her.

We rushed to her side and gently lifted her. After a moment, Mulligan straightened.
"She's cut her head on the stair corner. I suspect a mild concussion as well. If Faulkner wants to question her, he'll have to wait. She'll likely be unconscious for at least a week."

Jenny and Rose hurried to attend their mistress, and leaving her in their care, Mulligan stepped out of the clubhouse. He walked with his head lowered, brow furrowed. I stayed silent, but after a while I asked the question weighing on me:

"Do you think—despite everything—that Terence Foley might be innocent?"

Mulligan didn't respond immediately. After a long pause, he said, "It's possible, Lockhart. Just barely. One thing's certain— Faulkner has it all wrong. His conclusions are off from start to finish. If Terence is guilty, it's despite Faulkner's theory, not because of it. But the most damning evidence—the one thing that truly counts—is something only I am aware of."

"What is it?" I asked, genuinely intrigued.

"If you'd only engage your grey matter and see the case as I do, you'd spot it yourself," he replied.

It was one of those maddeningly cryptic responses he was fond of. But he didn't stop there.

"Let's walk toward the sea. There's a small rise overlooking the beach—we'll sit there and review everything. I'll tell you all I know. But I'd rather you reach the truth yourself than have me lead you to it."

We settled ourselves on the grassy knoll, gazing out over the waves.

"Think, my friend," Mulligan urged gently. "Arrange your thoughts. Be systematic. Be precise. That's where the key lies."

I did as he asked, sorting through the case detail by detail in my mind. And suddenly, a brilliant insight lit up my thoughts. I began piecing together my theory, hands trembling slightly.

"You've had a flash of inspiration, I see. Excellent—we're getting somewhere."

I sat up and struck a match for my pipe.
"Mulligan," I said, "it strikes me that we've overlooked something vital. I say *we*, though the real oversight may be mine. Still, your secrecy forced my hand. So, I say again—we've neglected someone."

"And who might that be?" Mulligan asked, his eyes twinkling.
"Caolan Reid!"

Chapter Twenty

In the next instant, Mulligan planted a warm kiss on my cheek. "Perfection! You've done it! And all on your own. It is magnificent! Go on with your reasoning—you are correct. Without a doubt, we made a mistake in overlooking Caolan Reid."

Flushed with pride from his praise, I found myself momentarily at a loss. But after gathering my thoughts, I pressed forward. "Caolan Reid vanished twenty years ago, but we've no actual proof he's dead."
"Not the slightest," Mulligan agreed. "Continue."
"Then let's assume he's alive."
"Exactly."
"Or at least that he was alive until recently."
"Agreed!"

"I propose," I said, warming to my theory, "that he fell into misfortune. Perhaps he became a criminal, a drifter, a thug—take your pick. He ends up in Magennis, and there he finds the woman he once loved and never forgot."
"Ah, ah! Careful with the sentiment," Mulligan warned.
"Where there's hatred, love often lingers," I offered, whether quoting or not. "In any case, he discovers her living under a different name. But now she has a new lover—Foley, the Englishman. Old resentments flare up. Reid confronts Foley and, consumed by jealousy and fury, stabs him. Panicked, he begins to dig a grave. I imagine Madam Wiffen comes looking for her lover, finds Reid, and there's a fierce confrontation. He drags her into the shed, and suddenly suffers an epileptic fit.

"Now suppose Terence Foley arrives. Madam Wiffen tells him everything, begging him to help—for the sake of her daughter's future, this past scandal must never come to light. The murderer is already dead—best to bury the truth with him. Terence agrees, goes to speak with his mother, and persuades her to go along with the story. Under Madam Wiffen's instruction, she allows herself to be tied up and gagged. That, Mulligan, is what I think happened."

I leaned back, glowing with the satisfaction of having constructed what I felt was a brilliant explanation.

Mulligan gave me a long, thoughtful look.
"My dear sir," he said finally, "you should consider writing for the cinema."
"You mean—?"
"It's an excellent plot. Would make a fine motion picture. But it bears not the slightest resemblance to real life."
"I admit I haven't worked out every detail—"
"You've gone beyond that—you've completely ignored them. What about the matter of clothing? Do you suggest Reid stabbed Foley, swapped outfits with him, and then put the murder weapon back in place?"

"I don't see how that matters," I said stiffly. "Perhaps he got money and clothes from Madam Wiffen earlier in the day—by threatening her."
"Threats, you say? You honestly suggest that?"
"Certainly. He could've threatened to expose her identity to the Foleys. That would have destroyed any chance of her daughter marrying Terence."

"You're mistaken, Lockhart. He couldn't have blackmailed her— she held the power. Caolan Reid is still a wanted man. One word from her and he'd be facing the guillotine."

I had to concede, albeit grudgingly, that he was right.

"And I suppose your theory accounts for everything?" I asked, a little tartly.

"My theory," Mulligan said calmly, "*is* the truth. And the truth, by definition, fits the facts. Your version went wrong at the start —you let your imagination run wild with secret meetings and emotional outbursts. But when dealing with crime, we must remain grounded in the ordinary. Shall I show you how I work?"

"Oh, please, do demonstrate!" I replied.

Mulligan sat up straight and began, wagging his finger for emphasis.

"I'll start where you did—with Caolan Reid. Now, remember the tale Madam Kinahan told in court about the 'Italians'? It was clearly false. If she wasn't involved in the crime, she made it up on her own, as she claimed. But if she *was* involved, then either she or Reid must have invented it.

"Now, consider this case. We see the same false story. As I said before, it's highly unlikely that Madam Wiffen invented it. So we look at the alternative: that the story originated with Caolan Reid. That fits. So Reid planned the crime, with Mrs Foley acting as accomplice. She's the visible figure in the case, but behind her is a shadowy presence—Reid himself, under some unknown alias.

"Now let's work through the Foley case step by step, placing each significant event in order. Do you have a notebook and pencil?"
"Yes, I do."
"Excellent. Let's begin. What's the earliest point to note?"
"The letter sent to you?"
"That was when we *became* involved—but it's not the real beginning. The first meaningful event was the change in Mr Foley's behavior soon after arriving in Magennis. Several witnesses noticed it. We must also take into account his relationship with Madam Wiffen, and the large sums of money he gave her.

"From there, we move directly to May 23rd."

Mulligan paused, cleared his throat, and motioned for me to write:

"23rd May. Mr Foley quarrels with his son over the latter's intention to marry Ciara Wiffen. Son departs for Belfast."

"**24th May**. Mr Foley changes his will, transferring full control of his estate to his wife.
7th June. He is seen quarreling with a tramp in the garden—witnessed by Ciara Wiffen.
A letter is sent to Mr Rupert Mulligan, urgently requesting help.
A telegram is sent to Mr Terence Foley, instructing him to travel to Lisbon aboard the *Esperanza*.
The chauffeur, Masters, is dismissed and sent on leave.
That evening, a woman visits. As he escorts her out, he is heard to say: 'Yes, yes—but for God's sake go now....'"

Mulligan paused here.
"Now then, Lockhart—take each of those facts one by one, examine them separately, and then together as a sequence. Do that and tell me if you don't begin to see this matter in a different light."

I tried my best to follow his instruction carefully. After a moment's consideration, I said hesitantly,
"With the early points, it seems to come down to a choice: was Mr Foley being blackmailed, or was he infatuated with this woman?"
"Blackmail—without a doubt. You heard Hall's account of Foley's character and behavior."
"But Mrs Foley didn't support that version," I pointed out.
"We already know Madam Foley's testimony is unreliable," Mulligan countered. "In this, we must rely on Hall's assessment."

"Still, Foley had an affair with a woman named Abbie, so it wouldn't be implausible if he had another with Madam Wiffen."

"True, I grant you that, Lockhart. But did he?"

"There's the letter, Mulligan. You're forgetting the letter."

"I forget nothing. But what makes you think that letter was meant for Mr Foley?"

"Well, it was found in his pocket and—and—"

"And that's your only evidence!" Mulligan interrupted. "No name, no addressee—just an assumption based on where it turned up: in the pocket of his overcoat. Now, do you remember what struck me about that overcoat?"

"You said it was unusually long. I thought you were just making conversation."

"Indeed? And later, you saw me measuring Terence Foley's overcoat as well. You noticed how short his was? Now consider a third fact: Terence left the clubhouse in haste on his way to Belfast. What do those three things suggest to you?"

"I see now," I said slowly, as realization dawned. "The letter wasn't meant for the father—it was written to Terence. In his rush, he grabbed the wrong overcoat."

Mulligan nodded approvingly.

"Exactly. We can come back to that point in more detail. For now, let's accept that the letter had nothing to do with Mr Foley senior and move on to the next event."

"**23rd May**," I read aloud. "Mr Foley has a heated argument with his son over the latter's intention to marry Ciara Wiffen. The son departs for Belfast."

"That seems simple enough," I added, "and the following day's alteration to the will was an obvious reaction to that quarrel."

"We agree on the cause, certainly," Mulligan said. "But what was Mr Foley's *real* motive in changing the will?"

I looked at him, puzzled.

"Well—anger, surely. He was furious with his son."

"And yet, he supposedly wrote affectionate letters to him

afterwards in Belfast?"

"That's what Terence claims. But he couldn't produce any of them."

"Exactly. So let's move on."

"Now we come to the day of the murder," I said. "You've listed events from that morning in a particular order. Are you sure of the sequence?"

"I've confirmed that the letter to me and the telegram to Terence were sent simultaneously. Masters was told shortly afterward he could take a holiday. I believe the quarrel with the tramp occurred earlier that same morning."

"You can't state that with certainty unless Madam Wiffen confirms it," Mulligan pointed out.

"No need—I'm convinced. And if you don't see the logic of it, Lockhart, then you're missing everything."

I stared at him, then suddenly the pieces fit together.

"Of course! I've been blind. If the tramp was Caolan Reid, it would've been after that confrontation that Mr Foley sensed real danger. He dismissed Masters—perhaps thinking he was in league with Reid—and then wired Terence, and wrote to you for help."

A flicker of a smile touched Mulligan's face.

"And don't you find it odd that he used the same wording in his letter that Madam Foley later used in her story? If 'Barcelona' was a red herring, why would Foley mention it—and even send his son there?"

"It's certainly confusing," I admitted. "Maybe we'll uncover the reason in time. But now we reach the evening—and the woman's visit. That still baffles me, unless Rose was right all along and the visitor was Madam Wiffen."

Mulligan shook his head.

"My dear Lockhart, where *is* your attention? Consider the torn cheque—and how Hall vaguely recognized the name Abbie Corrigan. Doesn't it now seem likely that *Abbie Corrigan* is the full name of Terence's unknown correspondent—and that it was she who came to the County Golf Course that night?

"Whether she intended to meet Terence or appeal directly to his father is unclear. But we can suppose what happened: she presented her claim—likely supported by letters from Terence. Mr Foley senior tried to pay her off with a cheque. She, deeply offended, tore it up. Her letter reads like one written by a woman truly in love—such a person would be insulted by money. In the end, Mr Foley got her to leave. And this, Lockhart, is where his final words are so revealing."

"'Yes, yes, but for God's sake go now,'" I repeated. "They just sound a bit intense to me, that's all."
"That's precisely the point," said Mulligan. "He was desperate for the girl to leave. And why? Not merely because the conversation was uncomfortable—no. It was because time was running out, and for some reason, that mattered a great deal."

"But why?" I asked, confused.
"That is the very question we must ask. Why should time have been so critical? Then, consider the matter of the wristwatch. That, too, emphasizes how vital the timing was in this crime.

"We're nearing the heart of the whole thing. We know that Abbie Corrigan left around 10:30, and from the wristwatch evidence, the crime occurred—or at least was staged—before midnight. We've now examined all the events leading up to the murder. Only one remains unaccounted for. According to the doctor, the tramp had been dead at least forty-eight hours when found—possibly as long as seventy-two.

"Now, based solely on the facts we've reviewed together, I conclude the death occurred on the morning of June 7th."

I stared at him, astonished.

"But how can you say that? What makes you so sure?"

"Because it's the only way the sequence of events makes sense. Lockhart, I've taken you along every step of this path. Can't you see what's glaringly obvious now?"

"My dear Mulligan, I see nothing glaring. I thought I was beginning to understand, but now I'm more lost than ever. Please—just tell me who killed Mr Foley."

"That," Mulligan said, "is the very thing I cannot say—not yet."
"But you just said it was perfectly clear!"
"We're talking at cross purposes, my friend. Don't forget—we're dealing with *two* crimes, and, as I mentioned before, we have the two bodies to prove it. Now, now—don't get all flustered. I'll explain everything.

"We must begin with psychology. We note three distinct moments where Mr Foley's behavior shifts significantly—three psychological turning points. The first takes place shortly after he arrives in Magennis. The second follows a quarrel with his son on a particular topic. The third occurs on the morning of June 7th.

"Now let's look for the causes. Number one likely stems from meeting Madam Wiffen. Number two ties into that, since it concerns the proposed marriage between his son and her daughter. But the cause of the third change remains hidden. That one we must work out for ourselves.

"Let me ask you something, Lockhart—who do we believe orchestrated this whole affair?"
"Caolan Reid," I replied cautiously, watching Mulligan closely.
"Exactly. Now remember what Faulkner said—that a woman lies to protect herself, the man she loves, or her child.

"Assuming Reid was behind the deception, and since he clearly isn't Terence Foley, we can dismiss the third motive. And since Reid isn't a woman, we can also rule out the first. That leaves the second reason: that Madam Foley lied to protect the man she loved—Caolan Reid. Do you follow?"

"Yes," I admitted. "That seems to hold up."

"Good. Then we can conclude that Madam Foley loved Caolan Reid. Now I ask you: who is Caolan Reid?"

"The tramp," I answered.

"Have we any evidence that Madam Foley loved the tramp?"

"No, but—"

"Then don't stick to a theory when the facts don't back it. Instead, ask yourself this: whom *did* Madam Foley love?"

I looked at him blankly.

"But you already know. Ask yourself—whose body caused her to faint dead away the moment she saw it?"

I blinked. "Her husband?" I gasped.

Mulligan nodded.

"Her husband—or, if you prefer, Caolan Reid."

I tried to push back.

"But that can't be. It's impossible."

"Impossible? Why? Didn't we just agree that Madam Wiffen was in a position to blackmail Caolan Reid?"

"Yes, but—"

"And didn't she in fact blackmail Mr Foley very effectively?"

"That's probably true, but—"

"And isn't it also a fact that we know nothing about Mr Foley's early life? That he simply appears out of nowhere, as an Irish-Australian, twenty-two years ago?"

"All that's correct," I admitted, a bit more firmly. "But you seem to be ignoring one major point."

"And what's that, Lockhart?"

"We've already agreed that Caolan Reid planned the crime. That would mean he planned his own murder. That's absurd."

Mulligan remained completely calm.

"Well, my good fellow," he said serenely, "that is exactly what he did."

Chapter Twenty One

In a calm and deliberate tone, Mulligan began to lay out his theory.

"It strikes you as odd, doesn't it, my good fellow—that a man would devise his own death? So strange, in fact, that you'd rather dismiss the truth as too far-fetched, clinging instead to a tale that is in reality ten times more unlikely. Yes, Mr Foley planned his own death—but there's one important point you may have overlooked: he never intended to die."

I shook my head, thoroughly perplexed.

"No, no—it's actually quite straightforward," Mulligan said kindly. "You see, the crime Mr Foley envisioned didn't require a murderer—only a corpse. Let's try to reconstruct the sequence, but this time from an entirely different perspective.

"Caolan Reid, fleeing the law, escapes to Australia. There, under a new identity, he marries and eventually amasses a vast fortune through investments in Spain. But despite his success, a longing for home takes hold. Twenty years have gone by; his appearance has changed significantly, and by now he is a man of standing. No one is likely to associate him with the fugitive he once was. He deems it safe to return.

"He settles in England but plans to spend his summers in Northern Ireland. And then—through misfortune, or perhaps fate's quiet justice—he ends up in Magennis. The one place in all Northern Ireland where lives the only person capable of recognising him. That person, of course, is Madam Wiffen.

"To her, he's struck gold—and she wastes no time in exploiting it. He's at her mercy, utterly powerless. She bleeds him for all she can get.

"Then comes the inevitable complication. Terence Foley falls in love with the lovely young woman he sees so often and wants to marry her. His father is aghast. At any cost, he must stop the match—he cannot allow his son to marry the daughter of the very woman who holds his darkest secret. Terence remains in the dark about his father's past, but Madam Foley knows the full truth. She's a woman of strong will, completely devoted to her husband. The two consult, and together they arrive at a desperate solution.

"Foley must vanish. He must seem to die, while in fact disappearing to start anew in some distant country under yet another identity. Madam Foley will stay behind, act the part of the grieving widow, and then join him later. But for her to have the necessary access to the fortune, the will must be changed—so he does exactly that.

"What they planned to use for a body, I cannot say—perhaps an anatomical skeleton burned in a fire. But before any firm plan is in place, something happens that changes everything. A ragged tramp, violent and aggressive, stumbles into the garden. A scuffle follows. Foley tries to throw him out. The man—an epileptic—collapses during the struggle and dies on the spot.

"Foley calls his wife. Together, they drag the body into the shed —the struggle had taken place just outside. It's an extraordinary opportunity. The dead man bears no real resemblance to Foley, but he's middle-aged, Irish-looking—ordinary enough to pass.

"I imagine they sat together on the bench just beyond earshot of the clubhouse, making their decision. The whole scheme comes together. Only Madam Foley will identify the body. Terence and the chauffeur—both of whom would notice any discrepancies— must be sent away. The household staff, being local women, are unlikely to come near the corpse, and even if they did, Foley would take steps to mislead them.

"Masters is packed off on holiday, a telegram is dispatched to Terence instructing him to go to Lisbon—a plausible enough story to support the fiction of Foley's sudden departure. Then Foley writes to me, having heard of me as a retired and obscure old investigator. He knows the letter, once shown to the examining magistrate, will lend credence to the narrative—which, indeed, it does.

"They dress the tramp in Foley's clothes and leave his tattered garments by the shed door—they dare not risk taking them into the clubhouse. Then, to lend authenticity to the tale Madam Foley is to tell, they drive the aeroplane dagger into the corpse's heart.

"That night, Foley will bind and gag his wife—he's learned from the past not to be too casual about the binding—and then head out with a spade. He digs a grave in the precise location where he knows a bunker is scheduled to be constructed. It's crucial that the body be found—Madam Wiffen must not suspect a thing. But by allowing a short delay before discovery, they reduce the chance of identifying the dead man.

"Once the burial is done, Foley puts on the tramp's rags and slips off toward the station, hoping to vanish on the 12:10 train. As the supposed murder will be timed for two hours later, suspicion will not fall on him.

"Now you understand his irritation at Abbie Corrigan's unexpected arrival. Every moment she lingered put his entire plan at risk. He dismissed her quickly. Then he returned to his preparations.

"He left the front door slightly open to suggest that his 'murderers' fled that way. He then tied up Madam Foley—correctly this time—repeating almost word-for-word the story from twenty-two years ago, unable to resist falling back on a script he'd used before.

"The air was chilly, and he pulled an overcoat on over his undergarments, intending to toss it into the grave with the body. He slipped out the window, carefully smoothing over the flowerbed, unintentionally leaving behind the clearest clue to his involvement. He crept onto the deserted golf course, spade in hand, and began to dig—

"And then—"

"Yes?"

"And then," Mulligan said solemnly, "the justice he managed to outrun for so many years finally caught up with him. An unseen hand struck him down from behind... Now, Lockhart, you see what I meant when I spoke of *two* crimes. The first—the crime Mr Foley, in his arrogance, invited us to investigate—is resolved. But behind it lies a more profound mystery. And that one has been far harder to untangle—because the killer cleverly used the scenario Mr Foley himself had staged. It's been a particularly challenging and intricate case."

"You're incredible, Mulligan," I said with genuine admiration. "Truly remarkable. No one else could have put it all together like this."

I think my praise affected him—he almost looked embarrassed. "Poor Faulkner," he said, attempting modesty. "It wasn't all incompetence on his part. He had some bad breaks. That strand of dark hair wrapped around the dagger, for instance—that was certainly misleading."

"To be honest, Mulligan," I said slowly, "even now I'm not sure I understand. Whose hair was it?"

"Madam Foley's, naturally. That's where Faulkner's misfortune came in. Her hair, though once dark, has turned nearly silver. Had that strand been gray, he never could have convinced himself it belonged to Terence. But of course, Faulkner's habit is always the same—bending the facts to suit the theory instead of the other way around.

"I've no doubt that once Madam Foley recovers, she'll speak. It probably never even occurred to her that her son might be suspected. Why should it? She believed he was already at sea aboard the *Esperanza*. Ah! That's a woman, Lockhart! What composure, what resolve! She only slipped once. When Terence showed up unexpectedly, she said, 'It does not matter—now.' No one caught the weight of those words. What an agonising role she has had to play.

"Imagine it—going to identify what she thought would be a vagrant dressed in her husband's clothes, only to find the real man lying dead before her. It's no wonder she collapsed. But since then, she has carried on with astonishing determination, concealing everything for the sake of her son. She can't risk anyone learning that Michael Foley was really Caolan Reid.

"And the bitterest irony? She had to publicly admit that Madam Wiffen was her husband's mistress—to fend off any suspicion of blackmail. A single suggestion of coercion might have exposed the truth. She handled the magistrate masterfully when he asked about Mr Foley's past. 'Nothing so romantic, I'm sure, sir.' That little touch of weary humour, the faint trace of mockery— it was perfect. It made Mr Andrews feel absurd for even asking. Yes, Lockhart, she's a remarkable woman. If she loved a criminal, she loved him nobly."

Mulligan fell silent, absorbed in thought.

"One more thing, Mulligan—what about the piece of lead piping?"
"You haven't worked it out? It was used to disfigure the victim's face—make identification impossible. That clue was what first put me on the right path. And that fool Faulkner, crawling all over the pipe looking for cigarette ends! Didn't I say a clue two feet long can be as valuable as one two inches long?

"Now we begin again. Who *killed* Michael Foley? The murderer must have been near the manor just before midnight, someone who stood to benefit from his death. That description fits Terence Foley all too well. The act may not have been premeditated.

"And don't forget—the dagger."

That jolted me. I hadn't fully considered it.
"Of course," I said. "The dagger in the tramp was the second one. So there were two of them?"
"Yes, and since they were identical, it follows that Terence must have owned them both. That detail doesn't bother me much, though. In fact, I had a small theory about that. But the most damning point is once again psychological. Heredity, Lockhart. Like father, like son—Terence Foley is, after all, the son of Caolan Reid."

His voice was calm but deeply serious, and despite myself, I was affected by his conviction.
"What was that little theory you mentioned?" I asked.

Instead of answering, Mulligan checked his large, old-fashioned watch, then asked,
"What time is the afternoon boat to Liverpool?"
"About five, I think."
"Excellent. That gives us just enough time."
"You're going to England?"
"Yes."
"But why?"
"To track down a potential witness."
"Who?"

Mulligan gave me a peculiar smile.
"Miss Abbie Corrigan."

"But how will you find her? What do you know about her?"

"I know almost nothing—but I have a few educated guesses. We can assume her real name is indeed Abbie Corrigan. Since Hall found the name vaguely familiar but couldn't connect it to the Foley family, it's likely she's in the theatre. Terence, a wealthy young man of twenty, probably met her on the stage—his first romantic entanglement, no doubt. That theory also explains why Foley senior tried to buy her off with a cheque. I believe I can locate her—especially with this."

He produced the photograph he had taken from Terence Foley's drawer. In the corner were the words "With love from Abbie." But that wasn't what transfixed me. The likeness, though imperfect, was clear enough.

I felt a cold dread settle over me, as if something unspeakable had just happened.

It was Belle.

Chapter Twenty Two

For a moment, I sat motionless, the photograph still clutched in my hand. Then, gathering my composure, I passed it back to Mulligan as casually as I could manage. At the same time, I cast a quick glance in his direction. Had he noticed anything? To my relief, he didn't seem to be paying attention to me at all. If anything in my reaction had struck him as odd, it had certainly escaped his notice.

He sprang to his feet with energy.
"We've no time to waste. We must depart immediately. All is well—the sea, she will be calm!"

Amid the rush and confusion of setting off, there was no opportunity for reflection. But once aboard the boat, away from Mulligan's watchful eye, I forced myself to think clearly and objectively. What did Mulligan actually know? Why was he so determined to find this girl? Did he suspect she had witnessed Terence committing the crime? Or was it possible—no, surely not! She had no motive, no grudge against Foley senior. There was no reason she would have wanted him dead.

So why had she returned to the scene of the crime?

I reviewed the known facts carefully. She must have alighted at King's Cross the day I parted from her. No wonder I hadn't found her on the boat. If she had dined near the station, then caught a train to Liverpool and boarded a boat to Belfast, she could have arrived at the County Golf Course at precisely the time Rose had described.

What had she done after leaving the clubhouse, just after ten?

Most likely, she either stayed the night in a hotel or returned to King's Cross. But then what? The murder took place on Tuesday night. Yet by Thursday morning, she was back in Magennis. Had she even left Northern Ireland? I was beginning to doubt it.

What had kept her there? A longing to see Terence Foley again? I had told her—as we had believed at the time—that he was already en route to Lisbon. But perhaps she knew that the *Esperanza* never sailed. If so, she must have seen Terence.

Was *that* what Mulligan was after?

Could it be that Terence, returning to see Ciara Wiffen, had instead encountered Abbie Corrigan—the very girl he had abandoned without a second thought?

The picture started to come into focus. If that were true, then her presence could offer Terence the alibi he so desperately needed. But then, why had he kept silent? Surely it would have been better to speak up. Was he afraid that this old fling would come to Ciara's ears?

I frowned, unconvinced. It had been a trivial, youthful romance. And frankly, I couldn't imagine a penniless Irish girl who still loved him refusing to keep his confidence. No, something didn't add up.

When we arrived in Liverpool, Mulligan was his usual brisk and cheerful self. The journey to London passed without incident. By the time we reached the city, it was just after nine o'clock, and I assumed we would retire for the night and begin our search in the morning.

But Mulligan had other ideas.

"No time to lose, my friend. The news of Terence's arrest won't hit the English papers until the day after tomorrow—but we must move quickly regardless."

I didn't quite follow his reasoning, but I simply asked how he intended to track down the girl.

"Do you remember Harold Prince, the theatrical agent? No? I helped him once with a peculiar case involving a Japanese wrestler. Delightful little conundrum—I must tell you about it someday. Prince will surely point us in the right direction."

It took some time to locate Mr. Prince, and it was past midnight by the time we succeeded. He greeted Mulligan warmly and assured us of his willingness to help in any way.

"There's not much in this business I don't know," he said, beaming.

"Well, Mr. Prince," said Mulligan, "we're looking for a young woman named Abbie Corrigan."
"Abbie Corrigan... I know that name, but I can't quite place her. What does she do?"
"I'm not sure—but here's her photograph."

Prince studied the image for a moment, and then his face lit up. "Of course! Got it!" He slapped his thigh. "The *Mairead & Abbie Kids*! That's who they are!"
"The *Mairead & Abbie Kids*?" Mulligan repeated.

"Yes! They're sisters. Singers, dancers, and a bit of acrobatics —quite a decent act. I believe they're out touring in the provinces right now—unless they're taking a break. They've been performing in Belfast for a few weeks."

"Could you find out exactly where they are at the moment?"
"Easiest thing in the world. You two go home and I'll send the details over in the morning."

True to his word, Prince came through. At around eleven the next morning, a hastily scribbled note arrived:
"The *Mairead & Abbie Sisters* are on at the New Theatre in Oxford. Best of luck to you."

Without delay, we set off for Oxford. Mulligan didn't ask any questions at the theatre. He simply purchased two tickets for that evening's variety show.

The performance itself was excruciatingly tedious—or perhaps it only felt that way due to the state of my nerves. Japanese family troupes balanced precariously on one another, dapper gentlemen in shiny evening wear and slicked-back hair delivered tired banter and tapped across the stage. Overweight sopranos strained their voices to the highest notes possible. A third-rate comedian attempted to imitate Billy Merson and failed miserably.

At last, the stage lights flickered and the placard announcing the *Mairead & Abbie Kids* appeared. My heart thudded with a sickening rhythm. And there she was—there they both were. One blonde, one dark, equal in height, dressed in short, frilly skirts and enormous "Buster Brown" bows. They looked like a pair of charming, mischievous children.

They began to sing. Their voices were fresh and true—somewhat thin and vaudeville in style, but undeniably appealing. The performance was light and lively. Their dancing was polished, their acrobatic tricks deft and well-rehearsed. The lyrics to their songs were bright and catchy. When the curtain fell, the applause was loud and well-deserved. The *Mairead & Abbie Kids* were clearly a hit.

But I could stand no more. I had to get outside. I needed air.

I leaned toward Mulligan. "I'm going," I whispered.

"By all means, my good sir," he replied. "I'm enjoying myself. I'll stay until the end and join you later."

It was only a few steps from the theatre to our hotel. I made my way up to the sitting room, ordered a gin and soda, and sat staring at the empty grate, my drink untouched, my thoughts spinning.

The door creaked open, and I looked up, expecting to see Mulligan. But it wasn't him.

It was Belle.

I sprang to my feet.

"I saw you—from the stage. You and your friend," she said, her voice uneven, her breath quick and shallow. "When you got up to go, I followed you. I waited outside and came after you. Why are you here—in Oxford? Why were you at the theatre tonight? Is the man with you... the detective?"

She stood there, wrapped in a cloak that had slipped slightly from her shoulders, revealing her stage costume. I saw the pallor beneath her makeup, heard the panic behind her words. And in that moment, it all fell into place. I understood—understood why Mulligan had come looking for her, understood what she feared, and at last understood the truth of my own feelings.

"Yes," I said gently.

Her eyes widened. "He's looking for... me?" she whispered.

When I didn't reply immediately, she collapsed beside the armchair and broke into a fit of harsh, bitter sobbing.

I knelt beside her, holding her close, smoothing her hair away from her face.
"Don't cry, child, don't cry... You're safe here. I'll protect you. I'll take care of you. Don't cry, Belle, don't cry. I know—I know everything."

She shook her head fiercely. "No, you don't!"

"I think I do." Her sobs began to ease, and after a moment I asked softly, "It was you who took the dagger, wasn't it?"

"Yes," she murmured.

"That's why you asked me to show you around that day? And

why you faked that fainting spell?"

She nodded again, wordlessly.

"Why did you take it?" I asked after a pause.

She answered with childlike simplicity. "I was afraid... afraid there might be fingerprints."

"But you were wearing gloves, weren't you?"

She looked confused, as if the thought had never occurred to her. Then, slowly, she said, "Are you going to—turn me in? To the police?"

"Good God, no."

She stared at me, her gaze long and searching. Then, in a small, trembling voice, she asked, "Why not?"

It was a strange time and place for a confession of love—nothing like I'd imagined it might be. But I answered simply, from the heart.

"Because I love you, Belle."

She bowed her head, overcome, and murmured brokenly, "You can't... not if you knew—" But then she straightened, summoning her courage, and looked at me directly. "What do you *know*, then?"

"I know you came to see Mr Foley that night. He offered you money, a cheque, and you tore it up. Then you left the clubhouse..." I hesitated.

"Yes?" she prompted.

"I don't know whether you were expecting to see Terence that night or just hoping to, or whether you wandered nearby out of sheer despair—but whatever the reason, you were still near the golf course around midnight. And you saw a man there..."

Again I paused. The truth had struck me the moment she walked into the room, but now the image grew even clearer. I saw again the strange design of the overcoat worn by the dead man. And I remembered the uncanny resemblance that had so startled me —when Terence himself had appeared, and for an instant I'd thought the corpse had come back to life.

"Go on," she said, her voice firm.

"I think he had his back to you. But you knew him—or thought you did. The walk, the way he carried himself, the pattern on his coat—you recognised it. You once wrote something to Terence, a veiled threat. And now, filled with rage and heartbreak, you lost control. You struck. I don't believe for a moment that you meant to kill him. But Belle—you did kill him."

She threw her hands up over her face and choked out, "You're right... you're right... I see it all now, just as you've said."

Then she turned on me with a kind of wild despair.

"And you *love* me? After all that—knowing what I've done—how can you say you love me?"

"I don't know," I said quietly, with a touch of weariness. "Love isn't something you choose. I've fought it, believe me, since the day we met. But it's stronger than I am. I love you, Belle. That's all I know."

Then, quite suddenly and without warning, she broke down again, collapsing to the floor in a fit of wild sobbing.

"Oh, I can't—I can't!" she cried out. "I don't know what to do. I don't know which way to turn. Oh, someone pity me—please— just tell me what to do!"

Once more, I knelt beside her, trying to calm her as gently as I could.

"Don't be afraid of me, Abbie. For God's sake, don't fear me. Yes, I love you—it's true—but I expect nothing from you in return. Just let me help you. Love him still, if you must—but let me be the one to help you now, in the way he never could."

It was as though my words had turned her to stone. She lifted her face from her hands and stared at me intently.

"You think that?" she whispered. "You think I still love Terence Foley?"

Then, with a sound that was part sob, part laughter, she flung her arms around my neck, pressing her tear-streaked face to mine.

"Not like I love you," she murmured. "Never the way I love you!"

Her lips brushed against my cheek, and then, finding mine, kissed me over and over with a fierce, sweet passion that left me breathless. The rawness of that moment—the wild, aching tenderness—I would never forget it. Not for the rest of my life.

It was the sound of the door opening that broke the spell. We both turned. Mulligan stood in the doorway, quietly watching us.

I acted without hesitation. In an instant I had reached him, grabbing his arms and pinning them to his sides.

"Quick," I said to Belle. "Go. Now. Get out while you can. I'll keep him here."

She gave me one final look—and then darted past us, disappearing down the hallway. I held Mulligan fast in my grip.

"My dear fellow," he said mildly, "you do this sort of thing exceptionally well. The strong man subdues his adversary—I am helpless as a child. But really, this is quite uncomfortable—and a little absurd. Shall we sit and talk like reasonable men?"

"You're not going after her?"

"Mother of Mercy, no! Do I look like Faulkner? Let go of me, my friend."

Keeping a wary eye on him—because I knew well enough that Mulligan's wits far outmatched mine—I loosened my grip. He eased down into an armchair, rubbing his arms tenderly.

"You have the strength of a bull when roused, Lockhart. But tell me—do you really think that was the right way to treat your old friend? I showed you her photograph, you recognised her instantly—and yet you said nothing."

"There was no need," I said coldly. "If you knew I recognised her, then what was the point of saying it aloud?"

"So! You didn't know that I knew that you knew," he said, with a wry smile. "And tonight you help her escape—after all our efforts to find her. Well then! It comes to this—are you working with me, Lockhart... or against me?"

I didn't reply right away. It pained me deeply to set myself against Mulligan. He had been my guide, my friend. But I knew where I now stood. I could not back away.

"Mulligan," I said quietly, "I'm sorry. I won't pretend I've been fair to you. But there are moments in life when you can't choose —when something chooses you. From this point on, I must follow my own path."

Mulligan nodded slowly, several times.

"I understand," he said softly. The mocking gleam was gone from his eyes, replaced with an unexpected warmth. "So it's come, has it? Love—not as you once imagined it, full of glitter and bravado, but sad, stumbling, bare-footed love. Ah, yes... I warned you, didn't I? When I realised the girl must have taken the dagger, I warned you. But by then it was already too late.

"Now tell me, how much do you actually know?"

I looked him directly in the eye.

"Nothing you could say would surprise me, Mulligan. I want you to understand that. But if you're thinking of going after Miss Corrigan again, I want you to be absolutely clear on one point. If you suspect she had anything to do with the murder—or that she was the mysterious woman who visited Mr Foley that night —you're wrong. I travelled back from Northern Ireland with her that day. I left her at King's Cross that same evening. So she *could not* have been in Magennis that night."

Mulligan studied me for a moment.

"And you would swear that in court?"

"I would," I said firmly.

Mulligan stood, bowed slightly, and said,
"My dear sir! Love conquers all. It works wonders. What a clever solution you've found. It even defeats Rupert Mulligan."

Chapter Twenty Three

After an intense moment such as the one I had just lived through, the inevitable reaction set in. That night, I went to bed feeling victorious—but by morning, the weight of reality returned. I was far from safe. True, the alibi I had hastily constructed seemed sound. So long as I stuck to it, I could see no way Abbie could be convicted.

But I knew I had to tread carefully. Mulligan wasn't the type to accept defeat without response. Somehow—at some time, and when I least expected it—he would try to turn the tables.

When we met over breakfast the next morning, we behaved as if nothing unusual had occurred. Mulligan's geniality remained unshaken, though I thought I detected a faint reserve that hadn't been there before. After we'd eaten, I casually announced that I was going out for a walk. A flicker of amusement lit Mulligan's eyes.

"If it's information you're after, there's no need to put yourself out," he said, with a teasing lilt. "I can tell you what you want to know. The *Mairead & Abbie Sisters* have cancelled their engagement and left Oxford—destination unknown."

"Is that so, Mulligan?"

"Take it from me," he replied. "I checked first thing this morning. What else did you expect?"

He was right, of course. Under the circumstances, Belle had done exactly what I'd hoped and planned for—she'd seized the small head start I'd secured for her and wasted no time in vanishing. It was what I wanted. Still, I found myself suddenly confronted by a fresh tangle of problems.

I had no means of contacting her, and yet she needed to hear the defence I had crafted in her favour—the story I was prepared to stand by. Perhaps she might try to get a message to me somehow, but I doubted it. She would know the risk of Mulligan intercepting it and resuming the hunt. No, she must simply vanish for the time being, without a trace.

But what was Mulligan planning? I studied him across the breakfast table. He wore an expression of utmost serenity, his gaze lost in the middle distance. It was a little *too* tranquil for comfort. With Mulligan, the more harmless he appeared, the more dangerous he usually was. His quietness made me uneasy.

Noticing the unease in my expression, he gave me a gentle, almost fatherly smile.

"You're puzzled, Lockhart?" he asked. "Wondering why I'm not rushing off in pursuit?"
"Well—something like that," I admitted.

"You see, that's what *you'd* do, were our roles reversed. I understand. But I don't care for chasing up and down the countryside after needles in haystacks, as your English say. No. Let Miss Abbie Corrigan vanish—for now. I'll find her when the time is right. Of that, you can be certain."

I looked at him warily. Was he bluffing? Or had he already gained the upper hand again? My earlier confidence was quickly draining. I had helped Abbie escape and invented a clever plan to protect her—but I could not bring myself to feel at ease. Mulligan's calmness made my nerves prickle.

"I suppose," I said hesitantly, "I've no right to ask what your next move is. I forfeited that."

"Not at all," he replied cheerfully. "There's no secret. We return to

Northern Ireland immediately."

"We?"

"Yes, *we*! You know perfectly well you can't afford to let Papa Mulligan out of your sight. Isn't that so, my friend? But stay in England, if you like—"

I shook my head. He was right, of course. I couldn't risk letting him go off on his own. Though he no longer trusted me, I could at least monitor his actions. The only real threat to Abbie came from Mulligan. Faulkner and the Irish authorities knew nothing of her—had no reason to. Mulligan alone had the power to put her in danger.

As this line of reasoning played out in my head, I saw Mulligan watching me with a satisfied little nod.

"I thought so. And frankly, I prefer it this way. Otherwise you might attempt to trail me with some ridiculous disguise—a false beard, perhaps. Everyone would notice, and I would be deeply embarrassed on your behalf."

"Very well, Mulligan," I said. "But I must warn you—"

"I know, I know—you're my enemy now. That doesn't trouble me in the least."

"So long as everything stays above board, I have no issue."

"Ah, that very English obsession with 'fair play!' Very noble. Since your conscience is satisfied, let's get moving. There's no time to lose. Our English visit has been brief but productive. I've learned exactly what I needed to."

He said it lightly, but something in his tone made me shiver. There was a hidden warning in the words.

"I still don't quite see—" I began, then broke off.

"Still, as you say," Mulligan echoed. "You're satisfied with your role. I, meanwhile, will turn my attention to Terence Foley."

The name hit me like a blow. I had all but forgotten him—Terence Foley, sitting in prison, facing the possibility of death under a false charge.

Suddenly, my part in the affair seemed far more grim. I could save Abbie, yes—but might that mean condemning an innocent man in her place?

The thought chilled me. I tried to shake it off. He would be acquitted. Of course he would. But doubt crept in again. What if he *wasn't*?

Could I bear the guilt of letting someone else pay with their life? Would it really come to that—choosing between Terence and Abbie?

The instinct in me screamed to protect the woman I loved, no matter the cost. But if that cost meant another's life—everything changed.

And what would *she* do if she knew? I hadn't told her about Terence's arrest. She had no idea her former lover was in a prison cell, facing a capital charge. Once she knew—what would she do? Would she sacrifice herself to save him?

She mustn't act recklessly. Perhaps Terence *would* be acquitted—without her having to intervene. That was the best outcome. But if he *wasn't*? That was the dreadful uncertainty.

Even if she were discovered, I doubted she would face the full severity of the law. Her crime was of passion, the result of jealousy, rage, provocation. She was young, beautiful—public sympathy would weigh in her favour. It had been a tragic mistake. She had believed she was striking down the son.

No—whatever happened, Abbie must be protected. And Terence Foley must not be condemned in her stead.

I didn't yet know how it could be done. But I trusted Mulligan. Somehow, he would find a way to save the boy—without revealing the girl. He had the skill to steer the truth just enough off-course.

Yes, I told myself again and again, it would end well. Abbie would remain free. Terence would be exonerated.

But beneath all my hopeful rationalisations, a chill lingered. A quiet, persistent dread.

Chapter Twenty Four

We crossed the sea that evening, and by the next morning, we found ourselves back in Belfast, where Terence Foley was being held. Mulligan wasted no time in arranging a visit to Mr Andrews. As he didn't seem inclined to object to my accompanying him, I joined him without question.

After the usual formalities and delays, we were shown into the examining magistrate's office. Mr Andrews greeted us warmly.

"I had been told you'd gone back to England, Mr Mulligan. I'm glad to see that report was mistaken."

"Oh, I did go," said Mulligan. "But it was just a quick trip—a sideline that I thought might be worth pursuing."

"And was it?"

Mulligan gave a noncommittal shrug. Mr Andrews sighed and nodded.

"We must face the facts, I fear. That man Faulkner—his manners are disgraceful, but he's no fool! It's hard to imagine him getting things wrong."

"You think so?" Mulligan asked quietly.

The magistrate shrugged in turn.

"Well, between ourselves—speaking confidentially—it's hard to see any other explanation, wouldn't you agree?"

"To be honest," said Mulligan, "there are still a good many unclear aspects to the case."

"Such as?"

But Mulligan wouldn't be drawn.

"I haven't organised my thoughts fully yet," he said. "Just a general impression. I liked the young man. I'd be sorry to believe him guilty of such a dreadful thing. By the way, has he said anything in his defence?"

The magistrate frowned, perplexed.

"I don't understand him. He offers no real defence at all. It's been difficult to get anything out of him. He denies the charge, yes— but beyond that, he lapses into an obstinate silence. I'm going to question him again tomorrow. Would you care to be present?"

We accepted the invitation with interest.

"It's a tragic business," the magistrate added with a sigh. "My heart goes out to Madam Foley."

"How is she?"

"She hasn't regained consciousness. In a way, perhaps, it's a mercy. She's being spared a great deal. The doctors assure me her life isn't in danger, but when she wakes, she'll need the utmost care. The shock, just as much as the fall, brought on her current state. If her mind were affected, it wouldn't surprise me in the least—not in the least."

Mr Andrews leaned back in his chair, shaking his head slowly and solemnly, as though savouring the tragic possibilities with a kind of gloomy relish. At length, he roused himself with a slight start.

"That reminds me—I've a letter for you, Mr Mulligan. Let me see, now... where did I put it?"

He began rummaging through his papers, eventually extracting the envelope and handing it over.

"It was sent to me to forward to you, but since you left no address, I was unable to send it on."

Mulligan took the envelope with mild curiosity. The handwriting was long, slanted, clearly foreign—and unmistakably feminine. But he didn't open it. Instead, he slipped it into his pocket and rose to leave.

"Well then, until tomorrow. Thank you again for your kindness and courtesy."

"Not at all. I'm always at your disposal."

We were just exiting the building when we ran straight into Faulkner. He looked more fastidious than ever, exuding confidence and satisfaction.

"Ah! Mr Mulligan!" he exclaimed brightly. "So, you *have* returned from England?"

"As you see," Mulligan replied coolly.

"I'd say the end of this case is near at hand."

"I agree," said Mulligan quietly.

Faulkner seemed delighted by Mulligan's subdued tone.

"What a poor excuse for a criminal! Not the faintest attempt at a defence—extraordinary!"

"So extraordinary," said Mulligan evenly, "that it certainly gives one pause, does it not?"

But Faulkner wasn't listening. He was already twirling his cane and grinning.

"Well then—good day, Mr Mulligan. I take it you're finally convinced of young Foley's guilt?"

"Not at all," said Mulligan. "Terence Foley is innocent."

Faulkner froze for a second—then burst out laughing. He tapped the side of his head with a smirk.

"Screwy!"

Mulligan straightened, and a dangerous glint sparked in his eyes.

"Mr Faulkner, your manner toward me throughout this case has been offensively disrespectful. It's clear you need a lesson. I'm prepared to wager you five hundred pounds that I identify the murderer of Michael Foley before you do. Do you accept?"

Faulkner stared at him, then repeated his earlier diagnosis: "Screwy!"

"Come now," said Mulligan, "is it a bet?"

"I have no wish to take your money."

"No fear of that—you won't win it."

"Well then, fine. Agreed. And for the record, your own manner has grated on me more than once."

"I'm delighted to hear it," said Mulligan pleasantly. "Good day, Mr Faulkner. Come along, Lockhart."

I followed him in silence. My mood was heavy. Mulligan had made his intentions clear—and they didn't bode well. That brief encounter had reignited his competitive spirit. I feared more than ever that I would not be able to shield Abbie from the consequences of what she'd done.

As we turned a corner, I felt a hand on my shoulder. I looked around to see Philip Hall. We stopped, greeted him, and he offered to accompany us on our walk back to the hotel.

"And what brings you here, Mr Hall?" Mulligan asked.

"One stands by one's friends," Hall replied dryly. "Especially when they're being falsely accused."

"So you don't believe Terence Foley committed the murder?" I asked eagerly.

"Not for a moment. I know the lad. I admit some aspects of this case have baffled me—but despite his foolish silence, I'll never believe that Terence Foley is a killer."

Hall's words stirred something deep within me. A weight I hadn't realised I was carrying seemed to lift.

"I'm sure many people feel the same as you do," I said earnestly. "There really is so little actual evidence against him. I should think his acquittal is all but certain—completely inevitable."

But Hall didn't share my confidence.

"I wish I could feel that way," he said quietly. Then he turned to Mulligan. "And you, sir? What do you make of it?"

"I think the case looks very bad for him," Mulligan said softly.

"So you believe he's guilty?" Hall asked, sharply.

"No. But I believe it will be extremely difficult for him to prove his innocence."

"He's behaving so damnably strangely," Hall muttered. "I know there's a lot more going on than meets the eye. Faulkner doesn't see it, of course—he's too far outside the circle. But the whole thing's been off from the beginning. Still, best not to go into that. If Mrs Foley wants to keep anything under wraps, I'll respect that. It's her affair, and I've got too much regard for her judgement to meddle. But I just can't understand Terence's behaviour. It's as if he *wants* to be found guilty."

"That's absurd," I burst out. "For one thing—the dagger—" I stopped short, uncertain how far I should go with Mulligan present. I chose my words cautiously. "We know Terence Foley didn't have the dagger in his possession that night. Mrs Foley knows that, too."

"That's true," said Hall. "And when she wakes, I imagine she'll have plenty to say. Well—I must leave you now."

"One moment," Mulligan said, halting him with a hand. "Would you be able to ensure I'm notified immediately if Madam Foley regains consciousness?"

"Certainly. That can be arranged."

As we headed up to our rooms, I turned to Mulligan.

"That point about the dagger—that was a strong one, wasn't it? I couldn't go into details in front of Hall."

"You did right," he said. "Let's keep that knowledge to ourselves as long as we can. But even then, I'm afraid it doesn't help us much. Do you remember I was gone for an hour that morning before we left London?"

"Yes?"

"I used that time to locate the firm that had made those souvenir daggers for Terence Foley. It wasn't difficult. And Lockhart, they didn't make two paper knives for him. They made three."

"So then—?"

"So then, one went to his mother, one to Miss Corrigan, and the third he must have kept for himself. No, the matter of the dagger won't get us out of this. It won't save him from the guillotine."

"That won't happen," I said sharply.

Mulligan gave a doubtful shake of the head.

"You'll save him," I insisted, more firmly now.

He glanced at me, eyebrows raised. "Haven't *you* already made that impossible, my good fellow?"

"There must be another way," I muttered.

"Ah, miracles now?" Mulligan said, lifting his hands. "But very well. Enough said. Let's look at this letter instead."

He drew the envelope from his pocket and opened it. As he read, a shadow passed over his face. Without a word, he handed the single thin sheet to me.

"There are other women suffering in this world, Lockhart," he said quietly.

The handwriting was shaky and distressed, clearly written in a moment of desperation.

Dear Mr Mulligan—
If you receive this, I beg you to come to my aid. I have no one else to turn to, and Terence *must* be saved. I am pleading with you—on my knees—to help us.
—Ciara Wiffen

I passed the note back to him, deeply moved.

"You'll go?"

"Immediately. Let's hire a car."

Half an hour later we arrived at Manor Carney. Ciara was waiting at the door and rushed to meet us, clutching Mulligan's hands tightly in hers.

"Oh, you've come—it's so kind of you. I've been desperate, not knowing what to do. They won't even let me see him in prison. I'm going mad. Is it true—what they're saying? That he isn't even denying the charge? That's madness. He couldn't have done it— he couldn't! I'll never believe it."

"Nor do I," said Mulligan gently.

"Then why won't he speak?" she cried. "I don't understand."

"Perhaps," said Mulligan slowly, studying her face, "because he's protecting someone else."

She frowned deeply.

"Protecting someone? You mean—his mother? I've suspected her from the beginning. Who inherits the whole fortune? She does. Easy enough to wear mourning and act the innocent. And when he was arrested, she collapsed, just like that!" She flung up her hands theatrically. "And that secretary—Hall—he's in it too. They're thick as thieves, those two. So what if she's older? Men don't care about that—especially if the woman's rich!"

There was bitterness in her voice.

"Mr Hall was in England," I said.

"So he claims. But who knows?"

"Madam," said Mulligan with quiet authority, "if you and I are to work together, we must start with clarity. May I ask you a question?"

"Yes, sir?"

"Do you know your mother's real name?"

Ciara looked at him for a long moment. Then, dropping her head into her arms, she broke into tears.

"There, there," said Mulligan gently, patting her shoulder. "I see you do know. Now a second question—did you know who Mr Foley really was?"

She raised her head and stared at him, startled. "Mr Foley?"

"Ah, no—you didn't know that. Then listen to me carefully."

And with that, he recounted the entire case to her, point by point, just as he had once done for me, back when we first departed for England. Ciara listened in silence, completely transfixed. When he finished, she inhaled sharply.

"You are amazing—magnificent! You're the greatest detective in the world!"

Then, with a sudden motion, she slipped from her chair and knelt before him, all emotion and abandon.

"Save him, sir," she cried. "I love him—I love him so much. Oh, please—save him! Save him!"

Chapter Twenty Five

We attended the examination of Terence Foley the next morning. Though only a short time had passed since we'd last seen him, the transformation in the young man was startling. His cheeks had hollowed, dark circles ringed his eyes, and he bore the haunted look of someone who hadn't slept for days. When we entered, he showed no sign of emotion.

"Foley," the magistrate began, "do you deny that you were in Magennis on the night of the murder?"

For a few seconds, Terence didn't respond. Then, in a voice strained and uncertain, he replied, "I—I told you I was at Belfast Port."

The magistrate turned briskly. "Bring in the station witnesses."

Moments later, the door opened, and in stepped a man I recognised as a porter from Magennis station.

"You were on duty the night of June 7th?"

"Yes, sir."

"You saw the 11:40 train arrive?"

"I did, sir."

"Look at the prisoner. Do you recognise him as having gotten off that train?"

"Yes, sir. That's Mr Terence Foley."

"You're quite certain? There's no possibility of a mistake?"

"None at all, sir. I know Mr Foley very well."

"And no doubt about the date?"

"No, sir. The murder was discovered the next morning, June 8th."

Another railway official was brought in. He confirmed the same details. The magistrate turned back to Foley.

"These men have positively identified you. Do you have anything to say?"

Terence simply shrugged.

"Nothing."

"Foley," the magistrate continued, reaching toward the table beside him, "do you recognise this?"

I stiffened. In his hand was the distinctive aeroplane-shaped dagger.

"Objection," cried Lord Brown, Terence's counsel. "My client must speak with me before responding."

But Terence brushed him aside and answered calmly, "Yes. I recognise it. It was a gift I gave to my mother—as a souvenir of the war."

"And to your knowledge," continued the magistrate, "does any identical copy of this dagger exist?"

Lord Brown again tried to interrupt, but Terence silenced him once more.

"Not that I know of," he said. "The design is my own."

Even the magistrate appeared momentarily taken aback by the audacity of that reply. It was clear that Terence was deliberately incriminating himself. I understood why—he was shielding Abbie. So long as the authorities believed there was only one such dagger, suspicion would never touch the girl who had held the second matching blade. He was protecting the woman he had once loved—at the gravest possible cost to himself.

I began to grasp the true enormity of the task I had so confidently placed on Mulligan's shoulders. Saving Terence Foley by any means short of revealing the truth now seemed near impossible.

The magistrate's tone grew colder, more cutting.

"Madam Foley insists that this dagger was on her dressing table the night of the murder. But then, she *is* his mother. You may find it surprising, Foley, but I consider it entirely plausible that Madam Foley was mistaken—that perhaps, inadvertently, you took the dagger with you to Belfast. Of course, you'll deny that —"

Terence's chained hands clenched tight. His brow broke out in sweat. Then, in a rasping voice, he cut in:

"I won't deny it. It's possible."

The room reeled. Even Lord Brown jumped to his feet in protest.

"My client is under extreme strain. I ask that it be recorded I do not consider him legally accountable for the statements he has just made."

Mr Andrews waved him down irritably. For a moment, he hesitated—as though a doubt had crept into his own mind. Terence had perhaps gone *too* far in playing the part of the guilty man. But the moment passed.

"Do you fully understand, Foley," the magistrate asked, leaning forward with emphasis, "that based on what you've just told me, I will have no choice but to commit you for trial?"

A flush of colour crept into Terence's otherwise pale face. He looked the magistrate squarely in the eye.

"Mr Andrews, I swear—I did not kill my father."

But the brief flicker of uncertainty had already faded from the magistrate's features. He gave a short, scornful laugh.

"They all say that, Mr Foley. Innocence—always claimed! But your own words condemn you. No defence. No alibi. Only the weak protest of a guilty man. You murdered your father—a vile, cowardly act—for the promise of an inheritance you believed you were entitled to. Your mother, I grant, may have aided you after the fact. No doubt the courts will show her a mercy you do not deserve. But your crime—your crime is repugnant to all decent men!"

He was interrupted.

The door burst open suddenly, and a flustered court attendant appeared in the doorway.

"Mr Andrews—sir—there's a lady—she says—she says—"

"Says what?" snapped the magistrate. "This is a flagrant breach of procedure. I forbid it—absolutely forbid it!"

But his protests went unheard. A slim figure in black stepped around the gendarme and walked into the room. A long veil obscured her face.

My heart sank. She had come, then. Despite everything, she had come. My efforts had been for nothing. And yet—even in my dread—I couldn't help but admire her bravery, the calm, determined way she entered that room.

She lifted her veil—and I gasped aloud. It wasn't Belle. Though the resemblance was uncanny, the girl standing before us was someone else entirely. And now, without the pale wig she had worn on stage, I instantly recognised her from the photo I had once found in Terence Foley's drawer.

"You are the examining magistrate, Mr Andrews?" she asked, her voice clear.

"Yes, but I absolutely forbid—"

"My name is Abbie Corrigan. I've come to confess to the murder of Mr Michael Foley."

Chapter Twenty Six

My friend—

You'll understand everything by the time this reaches you. Nothing I say will change Abbie's mind. She's gone—determined to give herself up. I'm too exhausted to fight her any longer.

You'll also realise now that I deceived you. Where you gave me your trust, I repaid you with lies. It might seem unforgivable. But before I vanish from your life completely, I wanted to explain how it all came to be. If I could know you'd forgiven me—just a little—it would make it easier to go on.

It was never about protecting myself. That's all I can offer in my defence.

It started on the day we met—on the train from Belfast. Even then, I was worried sick about Abbie. She was completely devoted to Terence Foley—would've let him walk all over her if he wanted. But he'd changed. The letters slowed. Something was off.

She became convinced there was another woman. And in the end, she was right. She made up her mind to go to their place at Magennis and confront him. I didn't want her to, and she tried to slip away without telling me. When she wasn't on the train at King's Cross, I knew something was wrong. I couldn't just carry on to England without knowing where she was. I had this awful sense that something terrible was going to happen if I didn't stop her.

I met the next train from Belfast. She was on it—and absolutely hell-bent on going to Magennis right away. I tried everything to dissuade her, but it was no use. She was tense and wild-eyed and wouldn't be reasoned with.

Eventually I gave up. I'd done all I could. It was getting late, so I went to a hotel. She went on. But that horrible, nagging feeling of dread stayed with me.

The next day came—no sign of her. She'd arranged to meet me at the hotel, but never showed. My anxiety grew worse. Then I picked up an evening paper... and saw the news.

I was devastated. Of course I couldn't *know*—but I had a terrible suspicion. I imagined her going to see Mr Foley, maybe confessing everything about her and Terence—and perhaps he insulted her, or worse. We both have fiery tempers.

Then all that nonsense about masked foreigners came out, and I began to breathe again. Still, the fact that Abbie hadn't kept our meeting haunted me.

By morning, I couldn't stand it any longer. I had to go and see for myself. And then I ran into you... well, you know what followed.

When I saw the dead man—dressed in that unmistakable coat of Terence's, with that eerily familiar face—I *knew*. And when I saw the paper knife—God, that horrible little thing!—I recognised it instantly. It was the one Terence had given to Abbie. And I couldn't help but think: what if her fingerprints were still on it?

That moment—I can't explain to you the panic and helplessness. There was only one thought in my head: I had to get that dagger out of there—before anyone noticed it was missing. I faked a faint. While you were off getting water, I snatched it and tucked it into my dress.

I told you I was staying at the Cherryhill Hotel—but that was a lie. I went straight back to King's Cross and caught the next boat to England. Out on the Irish Sea, I threw that wretched dagger overboard. Only then did I feel like I could breathe again.

Abbie was back in our London flat by then. She looked like death. I told her everything I'd done—and that, for the time being, she was safe. She just stared at me... and then started laughing. Laughing and laughing and laughing. It was awful.

I thought the best thing was to get her back to work. Keep her mind occupied. She'd fall apart if she had nothing to focus on. Fortunately, we got an engagement straight away.

And then, I saw you at the theatre. You and your friend. Watching us. I panicked. You must suspect something—or you wouldn't have found us. I followed you, desperate to know what you were thinking.

And then I realised—you thought *I* was Abbie. That I had taken the dagger.

If only you could've seen what was going on in my head then. Maybe then you'd forgive me. I was frightened, overwhelmed, and desperate. All I could think was that *you* might try to help *me*. But Abbie? I wasn't sure. Would you help her too? Or was it different? I couldn't risk it.

She's my twin. I had to do what I could for her. So I kept lying. I hated it. I still do.

And that's it. Enough, probably too much. I should've trusted you. I should've told the truth.

But once the news broke that Terence had been arrested, that was it. Abbie wouldn't wait for anything else.

I'm so tired now. I can't write more.

She'd started to sign it **Belle**, but crossed it out and wrote instead: **Mairead Corrigan**.

The handwriting was unsteady, tear-streaked, the paper worn soft at the creases. I still have that letter. I've kept it to this day.

Mulligan had been with me while I read it. The pages slipped from my fingers as I looked up at him.

"You knew the whole time—that it was the *other* one?" I asked.

"Yes, my friend."

"Why didn't you tell me?"

"At first, I couldn't believe you'd make such a mistake," Mulligan replied. "You'd seen the photograph. Yes, the sisters are strikingly alike—but not impossible to tell apart."

"But the blonde hair?"

"A stage wig. For contrast. Would it make sense that one twin would be naturally dark, the other fair?"

"Why didn't you say something that night at the Oxford hotel?"

"You weren't exactly... approachable," Mulligan said dryly. "You gave me no chance to speak."

"And afterwards?"

"Ah, well," he said more softly. "At first, I was hurt that you didn't trust me. Then I wanted to see if your... feelings would last. I wanted to know whether it was real, or just a passing whim. But I wouldn't have let you go on forever. I'd have told you soon."

I nodded. His tone was warm, forgiving. I couldn't hold it against him. I bent to pick up the letter again, then passed it across to him.

"Read it," I said. "I want you to."

He read it through in silence. When he finished, he looked up.

"What is it that's troubling you, Lockhart?"

His voice was gentler than I'd ever heard it. The teasing tone was gone. I could speak plainly.

"She doesn't say…" I hesitated. "She doesn't say if she loves me."

Mulligan turned back a few pages.

"You're wrong, Lockhart."

"Where?" I asked, leaning in.

He smiled faintly. "She tells you—in every single line of that letter."

"But how do I find her? There's no address. Only an Irish stamp."

"Don't worry," said Mulligan, rising to his feet. "Leave it to Rupert Mulligan. Give me five little minutes—and I'll find her."

Chapter Twenty Seven

"**C**ongratulations, Mr Terence," said Mulligan warmly, clasping the young man's hand.

Foley had come straight to us after his release, before returning to Magennis to see his mother and Ciara. Hall was with him, energetic and hearty—his mood a stark contrast to Terence's pallor and fatigue. The boy looked barely able to stand, haggard and hollow-eyed, as though teetering on the edge of collapse. He gave Mulligan a wan smile.

"I went through with it to protect her," he said quietly, "and now it was all for nothing."

"You couldn't seriously expect her to let you pay with your life," Hall said briskly. "She had no choice once she saw you were walking straight to the guillotine."

"And you *were*, too," added Mulligan with a flash of dry humour. "You'd have had Lord Brown's death from sheer indignation on your conscience if you'd kept going."

"He meant well, I suppose," said Terence wearily. "But he drove me mad. I couldn't exactly take him into my confidence. And now... what's going to happen to Abbie?"

"If I were you," said Mulligan, speaking plainly, "I wouldn't lose too much sleep over that just yet. The Irish courts are famously soft on youth, beauty, and crimes of passion. A good barrister will make a fine case for leniency. There'll be unpleasantness, no doubt—"

"I don't care about that," Terence interrupted. "The truth is, I feel responsible for my father's death. If I hadn't got involved with Abbie in the first place, he'd still be alive. And taking the wrong coat—my stupid mistake—that was what led to her mistaking him for me. I feel like I killed him, in a way. That guilt isn't going to leave me."

"No, no," I said gently, "you mustn't think like that."

"What hurts the most," Terence went on, "is knowing that Abbie's the one who killed him. But I treated her terribly. When I met Ciara and realised I'd been mistaken about my feelings, I should've written to Abbie. Told her the truth—openly and decently. But I was scared. Scared she'd cause a scene. Scared Ciara would find out and misunderstand. So I... just drifted. Hoping it would all sort itself out. I was a coward. And I drove her to desperation. If she'd stabbed *me* that night, I'd have deserved it.

"And the way she came forward in the end—that took real courage. I'd have seen it through to the end, you know. I was ready for it."

He fell silent for a while, lost in thought. Then he burst out with a new question:

"What I don't understand is—why was my father out on the links that night, wearing nothing but underwear and *my* coat? Was he trying to escape the people in the house? Or was the whole thing really a setup? Could it be—no, surely not—could my mother have actually believed it was me?"

Mulligan answered quickly. "No, no. She never thought that. You don't need to worry about that, Mr Terence. As for the rest—well, it's a strange story. I'll explain everything to you properly one day. But for now—will you tell us what happened that night, from your point of view?"

"There's not much to tell," said Terence. "I arrived from Belfast Port, just as I told you. I wanted to see Ciara before sailing away.

The train was late, so I took the shortcut across the golf links— it was easy enough to get into the Manor grounds that way. I'd nearly reached the house when—"

He paused, swallowing hard.

"Yes?" said Mulligan gently.

"I heard a terrible sound. Not loud—but a sort of gasp or choking cry. It terrified me. I stopped where I was, frozen. Then I crept around the side of a bush. The moon was out, and I saw a grave— freshly dug—and someone lying facedown, with a dagger in his back.

"And then—I saw her. She was staring at me like she'd seen a ghost. I suppose that's exactly what she *did* think, at first. Her whole face was frozen in horror. Then she let out a cry—and ran."

He stopped again, visibly shaken.

"And after that?" asked Mulligan.

"I don't remember very clearly. I think I stood there, dazed, for quite a while. Then it hit me—I needed to get away, fast. Not because I thought *I'd* be blamed, but because I couldn't bear the idea of being forced to give evidence against her. So I walked to the next town and hired a car back to Belfast Port."

A knock at the door interrupted us. A hotel pageboy stepped in, carrying a telegram. He handed it to Hall, who tore it open, read it, and stood.

"Mrs Foley is awake. She's regained consciousness."

Mulligan was already on his feet.

"Excellent! Let's all go to Magennis right away."

We moved quickly. Hall, after some persuasion from Terence, agreed to remain behind to help with anything concerning

Abbie Corrigan. The rest of us—Mulligan, Terence, and myself—piled into the Foley car.

The journey took just over forty minutes. As we neared the Manor Carney, Terence turned to Mulligan.

"Would you mind going in first—let my mother know I've been released? Soften the shock a bit."

"While you slip in quietly to find Madam Ciara?" said Mulligan with a knowing twinkle. "I was just about to suggest the same."

Terence didn't wait for more. As the car slowed, he jumped out and ran down the path toward the front door.

Mulligan and I continued on toward the County Golf Course.

"Mulligan," I said after a moment, "do you remember that first morning we arrived here? When we heard the news of Mr Foley's death?"

"Indeed I do," he said, glancing out the window. "It wasn't so long ago, was it? And yet—how much has changed since then. Especially for you, my friend!"

"Yes, indeed," I said with a sigh.

"You're speaking as a sentimentalist, Lockhart," Mulligan replied. "But I was referring to things professionally. We can hope the court shows Madam Abbie mercy. And after all, Terence Foley can't marry *both* girls, can he? But I speak as a detective. This case—this crime—is not cleanly done, not elegantly constructed. The staging—ah, yes! The masterpiece of Caolan Reid, that was impeccable. But the ending? A man dead, stabbed by a girl in a moment of rage? That's disorder. There's no symmetry in *that*."

I burst into laughter at the strange standards by which Mulligan judged murders. It was in that moment that Rose opened the door.

Mulligan quickly explained that he needed to see Mrs Foley immediately, and the old housekeeper led him upstairs. I stayed behind in the salon.

It was a long time before Mulligan came back down, and when he did, his face was unusually grave.

"Well," he said, "there it is, Lockhart. Lord help us, but we've got rough weather ahead."

"What do you mean?" I asked, startled.

He shook his head slowly. "I wouldn't have believed it. But women—women are full of surprises."

Just then, I glanced out the window.

"Look—here come Terence and Ciara."

Mulligan strode quickly to the front door, intercepting them on the steps.

"Wait. Don't go in. Your mother is very upset."

"I know," Terence said. "But I have to see her. I *must*."

"No, I advise against it. It would be better if you let me speak with her first."

"But Ciara and I—"

"In any case," said Mulligan firmly, "don't bring Madam Ciara with you. If you insist on going up, go alone. Trust me—it's for the best."

A voice echoed down the stairwell behind him, making us all jump.

"Thank you for your concern, Mr Mulligan—but I will speak for myself."

We turned to see Mrs Foley herself descending slowly, leaning on

Clare's arm. Her head was still wrapped in bandages. The young maid was tearfully urging her to go back to bed.

"You'll do yourself harm, Madam. The doctor said—please—"

But Mrs Foley continued her slow descent, resolute.

"Mother!" Terence cried, stepping forward. But she raised a hand, stopping him in his tracks.

"I am no mother of yours," she said coldly. "You are no son of mine. From this moment forward, I disown you."

"Mother!" he gasped, reeling from the blow.

For a heartbeat, she seemed to hesitate—perhaps some trace of pity stirred in her. Mulligan made a quiet gesture, trying to mediate. But she straightened again, proud and controlled.

"Your father's blood is on your hands. You are morally responsible for his death. You defied him for this girl, and your cruel treatment of another led directly to his end. Leave this house—this clubhouse. Tomorrow I will begin legal proceedings to ensure you never see a penny of your father's fortune. Make your way in the world if you can—with the help of the daughter of his most bitter enemy!"

And without another word, she turned and ascended the stairs, slow and dignified, Clare hovering anxiously behind her.

We stood in stunned silence, blindsided by the force of her words. Terence, visibly shaken after everything he'd endured, staggered and nearly collapsed. Mulligan and I caught him between us.

"He's done in," Mulligan murmured to Ciara. "He needs care. Where can we take him?"

"Home—to the Manor Carney," Ciara said at once. "My mother and I will look after him. Oh, Terence!"

We got him back to the manor, where he collapsed into a chair, barely conscious. Mulligan felt his forehead and hands.

"He's feverish. The strain of everything is finally catching up with him—and now this shock. He must get to bed at once. Lockhart and I will fetch a doctor."

One was found promptly, and after a thorough examination, he confirmed our fears.

"Exhaustion of the nerves. He needs absolute rest—no excitement. If left in peace, he'll likely recover quickly. But any further emotional upheaval might tip him into brain fever. Someone must stay with him through the night."

We left him in the care of Ciara and her mother and headed back to town. It was well past our usual dinner hour, and both of us were ravenous. The first restaurant we found offered a surprisingly good omelette and an equally good entrecôte.

When we'd finished—helped along by strong black coffee—Mulligan pushed back his chair.

"Now then, we need somewhere to sleep. Shall we return to our old friend, the Glenview Hotel?"

"Why not?" I agreed.

At the desk, they confirmed that two rooms with sea views were available. As Mulligan was taking the keys, he asked a question that took me by surprise.

"Has an English lady—Miss Robinson—checked in?"

"Yes, sir. She's in the small salon."

"Ah!"

"Mulligan!" I whispered as we followed the porter down the corridor. "Who is Miss Robinson?"

He turned to me with a twinkle in his eye.

"I've arranged your marriage, Lockhart."

"Wait—what?"

"Bah!" he said, chuckling and giving me a push through the doorway. "Do you think I'd announce the name *Corrigan* all over Magennis?"

It was Belle.

She rose as we entered, and I crossed the room in three strides, taking both her hands in mine. My eyes spoke for me.

Mulligan cleared his throat.

"My dear young friends, sentiment must wait. We have work to do. Madam—did you manage to do as I asked?"

Without a word, Belle opened her handbag and handed him a paper-wrapped bundle. Mulligan unwrapped it carefully.

I let out an involuntary gasp. It was the aeroplane dagger—the same one I had believed lost to the depths of the Irish Sea.

It struck me, not for the first time, how reluctant women are to truly destroy the things that might most incriminate them.

"Very good, child," said Mulligan approvingly. "You've done well. Now go and rest. Lockhart and I have some business to attend to. You'll see him tomorrow."

"Where are you going?" the girl asked, her eyes widening.
"You'll hear all about it tomorrow," came the reply.
"Because wherever you're headed, I'm coming too."
"But madam—"
"I said I'm coming too."
Mulligan quickly saw that arguing was pointless. He relented.
"Very well, madam. But be warned—it won't be entertaining. Most likely, nothing at all will come of it."

She didn't answer.

Twenty minutes later, we were on our way. Night had fallen completely, and the air was thick and stifling.
Mulligan led us out of town, taking the road that led toward the County Golf Course. But when we came upon Manor Carney, he stopped.
"I'd like to check in on Terence Foley—make sure he's still doing well. Come with me, Lockhart. Perhaps madam will wait outside. Madam Wiffen may say something that might upset her."

We unlatched the gate and made our way up the path. As we circled the building to the side of the clubhouse, I pointed out a window on the upper floor to Mulligan. A sharp silhouette stood out against the blind—Ciara Wiffen's profile.
"Ah!" Mulligan murmured. "I imagine that's the room where we'll find Terence Foley."

Madam Wiffen opened the door. She said Terence's condition hadn't changed, though we were welcome to see for ourselves. She brought us upstairs and into the bedroom. Ciara Wiffen sat at a table near a lamp, quietly working on some embroidery. As we entered, she raised a finger to her lips.
Terence was asleep, but it was a restless, uneasy slumber. His head turned from side to side, and his face remained unnaturally flushed.
"Is the doctor coming again?" Mulligan asked in a hushed voice.
"Not unless we send for him. Sleep is what he needs. I made him a tisane."

She returned to her needlework as we exited. Madam Wiffen came with us downstairs. Ever since I'd learned more of her background, I found myself observing her with growing fascination. She stood there, eyes lowered, the faintest, most enigmatic smile still playing on her lips. And suddenly, I felt a chill of fear—like the unease one feels in the presence of a beautiful yet venomous snake.

"I hope we haven't disturbed you, madam," Mulligan said politely as she held the door for us.

"Not at all, sir."

"By the way," Mulligan added as though struck by a passing thought, "Mr. Hall hasn't been in Magennis today, has he?"

I couldn't understand the purpose of the question, knowing full well it held no meaning for Mulligan.

Madam Wiffen answered calmly,

"Not that I'm aware of."

"He hasn't had a meeting with Madam Foley?"

"How would I know such a thing, sir?"

"Quite right," said Mulligan. "I just wondered if you'd seen him come or go, that's all. Goodnight, madam."

"But—" I began.

"No questions, Lockhart. There'll be time for those later."

We rejoined Belle and made our way briskly toward the County Golf Course. Mulligan cast one glance back at the lit window, where Ciara's profile still bent intently over her work.

"At least he's being watched over," he muttered.

Once at the golf course, Mulligan led us to a cluster of bushes off to the left of the drive. From there, we had a clear view of the manor while remaining completely concealed. The building itself was cloaked in darkness. It seemed safe to assume that everyone was asleep.

We had stationed ourselves just beneath the window of Mrs. Foley's bedroom, which I noticed was open. Mulligan's gaze seemed fixed on that very spot.

"What exactly are we doing?" I whispered.

"Waiting."

"But—"

"I don't expect anything for an hour at least, maybe two. But the —"

His sentence was cut off by a piercing, drawn-out cry:

"Help!"

A light flared on in a second-floor room to the right of the main entrance. The cry had come from there. As we looked up, a silhouette appeared on the blind—two people seemed to be locked in a struggle.

"Good lord!" Mulligan exclaimed. "She must've changed rooms."

He bolted forward, pounding furiously on the front door. Then he darted over to the tree by the flower bed and climbed it like a cat. I hurried after him as he leapt through the open window. Glancing back, I saw Mairead just grabbing hold of a branch.

"Be careful!" I shouted.

"Worry about yourself!" she shot back. "This is easy for me."

Inside, Mulligan raced through the vacant room and hammered at the inner door.

"Locked and bolted from the outside," he snarled. "It'll take time to break through."

The cries from inside were growing weaker by the second. I could see the desperation in Mulligan's face. He and I threw our shoulders against the door.

Belle's voice came from the window—calm and matter-of-fact: "You'll be too late. Looks like I'm the only one who can help."

Before I could stop her, she launched herself from the window into the night. I ran over and looked down, horrified to see her hanging from the roof by her hands, inching her way toward the illuminated window.

"My God! She'll fall," I cried.

"You forget—she's a professional acrobat, Lockhart. Thank heaven she insisted on coming. I only hope she's not too late. Ah!"

A scream of sheer terror echoed into the night just as Belle vanished through the window. Then came her firm, clear voice: "No, you don't! I've got you—and my wrists are like steel."

At that moment, the door we were trapped behind creaked open. Rose stood there. Mulligan pushed past her without a word and sprinted down the hall, where the maids were huddled near another door.

"It's locked from the inside, sir."

We heard a heavy thud from within. Moments later, a key turned, and the door slowly swung open. Belle stood there, pale, and waved us in.

"She's safe?" Mulligan demanded.

"Yes. I reached her just in time. She was completely spent."

Mrs. Foley lay half-upright on the bed, gasping.

"She tried to strangle me," she whispered hoarsely.

Belle stooped to pick something off the floor and handed it to Mulligan. It was a tightly rolled ladder made of fine but strong silk rope.

"A getaway plan," said Mulligan. "Through the window—while we were breaking down the door. And where's—the other?"

Belle stepped aside and pointed. A figure lay crumpled on the floor, wrapped in dark fabric, the face obscured.

"Dead?" She nodded.

"I think so. Probably hit her head on the marble hearth."

"But who is it?" I gasped.

"The one who murdered Foley," Mulligan said gravely. "And who just tried to murder Madam Foley."

Baffled and stunned, I knelt down, lifted the cloth—and found myself staring into the lifeless yet still strikingly beautiful face of Ciara Wiffen.

Chapter Twenty Eight

My recollections of the later events that night are muddled and indistinct. Mulligan paid no attention to my repeated questions —he seemed deaf to them entirely. He was instead directing his full energy toward berating Rose for failing to inform him that Mrs. Foley had changed bedrooms.

I seized him by the shoulder, determined to break through his distraction and force him to listen.

"But you must have known," I insisted. "You were taken up to see her earlier this afternoon."

Mulligan deigned to acknowledge me for the briefest of moments.

"She'd been wheeled into the centre room—her boudoir," he clarified.

"But sir," Rose interrupted, "Madam moved to another room almost immediately after the murders. The memories—they were too painful!"

"Then why on earth wasn't I told?" Mulligan bellowed, slamming his hand on the table as his temper surged. "Answer me—why—was—I—not—informed? You're an old woman, completely senile! And Clare and Jenny are just as hopeless. The lot of you—utter fools! Your incompetence nearly cost your mistress her life. If it weren't for this brave young woman—"

He broke off mid-rant, then darted across the room to where the girl was tending to Mrs. Foley and embraced her with unmistakable Irish enthusiasm—an act that, I must admit, stirred a pang of irritation in me.

My foggy mental state was abruptly shattered when Mulligan barked an order at me: fetch the doctor immediately, for Mrs. Foley. After that, I was to summon the police. Then, as if to add insult to injury, he added:

"There's no point in you returning here. I'll be too occupied to speak with you, and as for Madam here—I'm assigning her as nurse."

With what little dignity I could muster, I withdrew. I completed my errands and returned to the hotel, my head reeling. I could make neither head nor tail of the night's events. Everything felt surreal—like something out of a fevered imagination. No one would answer my questions. No one even seemed to hear them. Frustrated and drained, I threw myself into bed and slept the sleep of the confused and thoroughly worn out.

When I awoke, sunlight was streaming in through the open windows—and there sat Mulligan beside the bed, fresh, composed, and smiling.

"Finally, you're awake! You really are a champion sleeper, Lockhart. Do you realise it's almost eleven?"

I groaned, raising a hand to my throbbing head.

"I must've been dreaming," I said groggily. "I actually dreamt we found Ciara Wiffen's body in Mrs. Foley's room—and that you claimed she murdered Mr. Foley."

"You weren't dreaming. That all happened."

"But I thought Abbie Corrigan was the one who killed Mr. Foley?"

"Oh no, Lockhart. She merely said that—to protect the man she loved from the guillotine."

"What?"

"Think back to Terence Foley's story. They both arrived at the scene at the exact same time, and each assumed the other had committed the crime. The girl, horrified, fled the moment she saw him. But when she learned that suspicion had fallen on him, and that he might be sentenced to death, she couldn't stand by and let that happen. So she stepped forward, falsely confessed, and tried to save him."

Mulligan leaned back in his chair and steepled his fingers in that familiar thoughtful gesture of his.

"I was never quite satisfied with the case as it stood," he said in a judicious tone. "From the start, I suspected we were dealing with a cold-blooded, carefully planned murder—one where the killer cleverly borrowed Foley's own scheme to throw off the police. As I've told you before, Lockhart—the most successful criminals are almost always disarmingly simple."

I gave a nod of agreement.

"To support that theory," he went on, "the murderer would have had to know the full details of Foley's plans. That brought my suspicions to Mrs. Foley. But there simply wasn't any evidence to support the idea that she was guilty. So who else might have known about the scheme? Well—Ciara Wiffen herself told us she overheard Foley's argument with the tramp. If she could catch that, why not the rest—especially if the Foleys were careless enough to discuss their plan while sitting on the bench? Think how easily you overheard Ciara's conversation with Terence from that same place."

"But what motive could Ciara possibly have had to kill Mr. Foley?" I asked. "Why would she do it?"

"Motive? Money!" Mulligan exclaimed. "Foley was a multi-millionaire. At his death—or so she and Terence believed—half that fortune would go to his son. Let's walk through the situation from Ciara Wiffen's point of view.

"She overhears the discussion between Foley and his wife. Up to now, she and her mother have been extracting a tidy income from him. But now he's looking to break free. At first, she may only wish to prevent him from cutting them off. But soon, a more daring idea forms—one that wouldn't shock the daughter of Lisa Kinahan in the slightest!

"Right now, Foley is the main obstacle to her marriage with Terence. If Terence defies his father and marries her, he's cut off without a penny—something Madam Ciara finds utterly unacceptable. In fact, I doubt she ever truly cared for Terence. She knew how to play emotions well enough, but she had the same cold, calculating nature as her mother. And I suspect she wasn't at all confident she could hold his affections if they were separated—which his father could easily arrange.

"But if Foley dies, and Terence becomes heir to his millions? The marriage can proceed immediately, and she gains immense wealth—not the pathetic thousands she's scraped together so far.

"Her cunning mind sees the perfect opportunity. Foley has already set the stage for his fake murder. All she needs to do is act at the right moment—and transform his illusion into grim truth.

"And here's the clincher—the second clue that led me straight to her: the dagger!

"Foley had three replicas made. He gave one to his mother, another to Abbie Corrigan—and don't you think it's highly likely that he gave the third to Ciara Wiffen?"

"So, to sum it all up," Mulligan said, "there were four key reasons to suspect Ciara Wiffen:

First, she could easily have overheard Foley discussing his plans. Second, she had a strong personal motive for wanting him dead.

Third, she was the daughter of the infamous Madam Kinahan, who—if you ask me—was morally and effectively responsible for her husband's death, even if it was Caolan Reid who delivered the final blow.

And fourth, she was the only person, aside from Terence Foley, who likely had possession of the third souvenir dagger."

Mulligan paused to clear his throat.

"Now, once I discovered the existence of the other girl—Abbie Corrigan—I saw that it was entirely possible she might have been the one who killed Foley. I didn't much like that outcome, mind you—because, as I've told you before, Lockhart, a man of my expertise enjoys facing a criminal who's truly a match for him. Still, one must accept crimes as they are, not as one wishes them to be. It seemed unlikely that Abbie would be wandering around with a keepsake paper-knife in her hand, but then again, she might have been harbouring thoughts of revenge against Terence all along. When she stepped forward and confessed, it appeared to be the end of it.

"But still—I wasn't convinced. I couldn't settle with it...

"So I went over the whole thing again—every detail—and I came right back to the same conclusion: if it wasn't Abbie Corrigan, then the only person it could possibly be was Ciara Wiffen. And yet—I had *nothing*. Not a single piece of real evidence!

"And then you handed me that letter from Madam Mairead—and suddenly, I saw a way to close the net.

"You see, the original dagger was taken by Mairead Corrigan and thrown into the sea—believing, naturally, that it had belonged to her sister. But if, by chance, it wasn't Abbie's dagger, but the one Terence had given to Ciara Wiffen—well then, Abbie's would still be among her belongings. That would be the proof I needed!

"I didn't say a word to you at the time, Lockhart—it wasn't the moment for sentiment—but I tracked down Madam Mairead, told her only what was necessary, and instructed her to search her sister's things. Just imagine my delight when she came to me, just as planned, under the name of Miss Robinson, carrying the dagger!"

"In the meantime," Mulligan continued, "I had taken steps to drive Madam Ciara out into the open. Acting on my instructions, Madam Foley turned her son away, and told him she would be changing her will the next day to ensure he received none of his father's estate. It was a risky tactic, but a vital one. Madam Foley knew the stakes and agreed to go through with it—though, unfortunately, she neglected to mention that she had changed rooms. I suppose she assumed I already knew. Everything unfolded just as I'd anticipated.

"Ciara Wiffen made one final, desperate attempt to secure the Foley fortune—and she failed."

"What completely baffles me," I said, "is how she managed to get into the clubhouse without us seeing her. It seems impossible! We left her behind at the Manor Carney, went directly to the County Golf Course—and yet somehow, she was already there."

"Ah," Mulligan said, "but we didn't really leave her behind. While we were speaking with her mother in the hallway, she slipped out through the back. That's where—if I may borrow from our American friends—she 'pulled a fast one' on Rupert Mulligan!"

"But what about the silhouette we saw on the blind? We all saw it from the road."

"Ah, yes. By the time we looked up, Madam Wiffen had just enough time to hurry upstairs and take her daughter's place."

"Madam Wiffen?"

"Yes. One is older, the other younger—one dark, one fair—but when it comes to casting a silhouette on a drawn blind, their profiles are strikingly similar. Even I didn't notice the difference

—triple fool that I was! I believed I still had time before Ciara would try to enter the manor. I underestimated her. She was clever—that Madam Ciara."

"And her plan was to murder Mrs. Foley?"

"Exactly. The entire estate would then pass to her son. But the way she planned to do it—Lockhart—it would have looked like suicide. Beside Ciara Wiffen's body, I found a small notepad, a vial of chloroform, and a hypodermic needle filled with a lethal dose of morphine. You see? Chloroform first—then, once the victim is unconscious, a quick injection. By morning, the scent of the chloroform would be gone, and the syringe would appear to have fallen from Madam Foley's own hand.

"And what would the esteemed Mr. Andrews have said? 'Poor woman! I warned you, didn't I? The shock of joy—too much for her, given everything she'd been through. I would not be surprised if her mind simply gave way. A tragic case—the Foley Case!'"

Mulligan shook his head.

"But things didn't go according to Ciara's design. For starters, Madam Foley was awake—waiting. They struggled. But Mrs. Foley was still very weak. Ciara saw that her suicide plan was ruined. Her last hope lay in silencing Madam Foley with her bare hands, escaping with the rope ladder while we were still trying to break through the far door, and making it back to the Manor Carney before we returned. If she could pull that off, it would be very difficult to prove anything against her.

"But she didn't count on one thing: being stopped—not by me, Rupert Mulligan—but by the little acrobat with wrists like steel."

I sat quietly, turning over the full weight of the story in my mind.

"When did you first begin to suspect Ciara Wiffen, Mulligan?

Was it when she mentioned overhearing the argument in the garden?"

Mulligan smiled.

"My friend, do you remember the day we first arrived in Magennis? That beautiful girl standing by the gate? You asked me if I noticed the young goddess—and I told you I'd seen only a girl with anxious eyes. That's how I've thought of Ciara Wiffen ever since. The girl with the anxious eyes.

"And why was she anxious? Not on Terence Foley's account— because she hadn't yet learned that he'd been in Magennis the night before."

"By the way," I asked suddenly, "how is Terence Foley?"

"He's improving. Still staying at Manor Carney. But Madam Wiffen has vanished. The police are actively searching for her."

"Do you think she was working with her daughter?"

"We'll likely never know. Madam Wiffen is a woman who keeps her secrets well. And I sincerely doubt the police will ever track her down."

"Has anyone told Terence the truth?"

"Not yet."

"It's going to be a brutal shock for him."

"Undoubtedly. And yet, Lockhart, I find myself wondering if his heart was ever truly involved. Up to now, we've been thinking of Abbie Corrigan as the temptress, and Ciara Wiffen as the one he truly loved. But what if it was the other way around? Ciara was extraordinarily beautiful—she made it her mission to bewitch Terence, and she succeeded. But consider his peculiar reluctance to sever ties with the other girl. Remember how he was willing to face execution rather than let her be implicated? I have a hunch that, once he knows the truth, he'll be repelled—

his infatuation will crumble."

"What about Faulkner?"

"That poor man's had a nervous breakdown! He had to return to Belfast."

We both chuckled.

As it turned out, Mulligan's prediction wasn't far off. When the doctor finally declared Terence strong enough to bear the truth, it was Mulligan who took on the task of breaking it to him. The blow was heavy, but Terence handled it better than I'd imagined possible. His mother's unwavering devotion carried him through those harrowing days—they were now inseparable.

There was still one more revelation to be made. Mulligan had informed Mrs. Foley that he knew her secret and urged her not to withhold the truth from Terence.

"To bury the past does no good, madam. Be brave—tell him everything."

With a heavy heart, she agreed, and Terence finally learned that the father he had revered had, in reality, been a fugitive from the law. A faltering question from the boy was quickly answered by Mulligan.

"Rest easy, Mr. Terence. The world knows nothing. As far as I can see, I'm under no obligation to speak to the police. From beginning to end, I acted on behalf of your father—not the authorities. Justice found him in the end, but there's no need for anyone to learn that Caolan Reid and your father were one and the same."

There were, of course, certain unresolved points in the case that continued to puzzle the local police. But Mulligan offered explanations so smooth and plausible that, eventually, all questions faded away.

Some time after we'd returned to London, I noticed an impressive model of a foxhound displayed proudly on Mulligan's mantel. He caught my curious look and gave a knowing nod.

"But of course! I received my five hundred pounds. Isn't he a fine fellow? I've named him Faulkner!"

A few days later, Terence Foley paid us a visit. His expression was firm, decisive.

"Mr. Mulligan," he said, "I've come to say goodbye. I'll be sailing for Spain shortly. My father had significant business interests on the continent, and I intend to begin a new chapter there."

"You're going alone, Mr. Terence?"

"My mother's coming with me. And I plan to keep Hall on as my secretary. He enjoys remote places."

"No one else? Not even—"

Terence flushed.

"You mean—?"

"A young woman who loves you deeply, who would have laid down her life for you."

"How can I ask her?" he muttered. "After everything that's happened—how could I face her? What could I possibly say that wouldn't sound hollow?"

"Women," Mulligan said, "have a remarkable talent for finding ways to prop up broken stories."

"Yes, but—I've behaved like a complete fool."

"As have we all, from time to time," Mulligan replied, with his usual calm wisdom.

But Terence's face had grown more serious.

"There's something else. I'm my father's son. Who would marry me with that knowledge hanging over me?"

"You claim to be your father's son. Lockhart here will tell you—I believe heredity carries weight."

"Then—"

"Wait. I also know a woman. A woman of strength and endurance. A woman capable of deep love and extraordinary sacrifice."

Terence's gaze lifted. His eyes softened.

"My mother."

"Yes. You're as much your mother's son as your father's. So go to Madam Abbie. Be honest. Tell her everything. Don't hide a single truth—and see what she says."

Terence hesitated, visibly torn.

"Go to her not as a boy, but as a man. A man shaped by the burden of the past and the weight of the present—but one who's ready to build something new and extraordinary. Ask her to share it with you. You may not realise it, but your love for each other has been tested—by fire—and it has not failed. You've both been willing to give your lives for each other."

And what of Captain Seamus Lockhart, humble narrator of these events?

There's talk he might join the Foleys on a ranch across the sea, but I prefer to end this tale where it began—in the garden of the County Golf Course, on a quiet morning.

"I can't call you Abbie," I said, "because that's not really your name. And 'Mairead' feels too formal. So it has to be Belle. Belle married the Beast, remember—and he became a prince. I'm not a prince, but—"

She cut me off.

"Belle warned him, I'm sure. She couldn't promise to turn into a princess. She was just a little scullery maid, after all—"

"Then it's the prince's turn to interrupt," I said quickly. "Do you know what he said?"

"No?"

"'Hell!' said the prince—and kissed her."

And I did just that.

About The Author

Chris Franklin

Chris Franklin is a crime thriller author based in regional Victoria, Australia, where he crafts gripping tales that transport readers to the heart of danger and suspense. Originally hailing from Queensland, Chris's fascination with both fiction and true crime fuels his vivid storytelling, weaving intricate plots inspired by his love for the genre. When he's not immersed in crime stories, Chris can be found exploring the wide open roads of Australia  or enjoying the outdoors with his large black dog by his side. His passion for travel and adventure echoes through his writing, offering readers a thrilling journey in every book.

www.bigstretchpublishing.com

Books By This Author

Fire At Four Ways

Dire Warning

Countdown To Deadfall

www.ingramcontent.com/pod-product-compliance
Lightning Source LLC
Chambersburg PA
CBHW060427180626
46817CB00007B/2694